Dear God. Why did she have to end up with a hockey player?

"Stop looking at me like that." Hayden glared.

"Like what?" Brody said, blinking innocently.

"Like you're imagining me naked."

"I can't help it. I *am* imagining you naked."

His eyes darkened to a glitter, and liquid heat pooled between her thighs. She tried not to squeeze her legs together.

"I told you this morning I wanted to leave things at one night," she protested.

He moved closer, his lips inches from her ear, his warm breath fanning her neck. "What about what I want?"

She resisted the urge to moan. If she wasn't careful she'd hop right back into bed with Brody Croft.

And she'd love every sexy second of it....

Blaze

Dear Reader,

I am absolutely thrilled about writing for Harlequin Blaze. *Body Check* is a story that's been in my head for quite a while. It's a dream come true to be able to share it with you!

Growing up in Canada, I suppose it's not surprising that I ended up writing about our nation's most beloved sport. After all, there's nothing sexier than a hockey player. And, of course, no romance would be complete without a scandal or two!

I had a blast writing *Body Check,* from its initial conception to the research phase (where I pestered my hockey-playing buddies with questions ike "What *really* goes on in the locker room?") to those final, finishing touches.

I hope you enjoy Hayden and Brody's story, and I'd also love to hear from you! Drop me a line at www.ellekennedy.com or swing over to The Sizzling Pens at sizzlingpens.blogspot.com to see what some of my fellow Harlequin authors and I are blogging about!

Happy reading!

Elle Kennedy

Body Check

ELLE KENNEDY

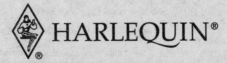

TORONTO • NEW YORK • LONDON
AMSTERDAM • PARIS • SYDNEY • HAMBURG
STOCKHOLM • ATHENS • TOKYO • MILAN • MADRID
PRAGUE • WARSAW • BUDAPEST • AUCKLAND

Recycling programs for this product may not exist in your area.

ISBN-13: 978-0-373-79462-1
ISBN-10:   0-373-79462-2

BODY CHECK

This edition published by arrangement with Harlequin Books S.A.

® and TM are trademarks of the publisher. Trademarks indicated with ® are registered in the United States Patent and Trademark Office, the Canadian Trade Marks Office and in other countries.

www.eHarlequin.com

Printed in U.S.A.

ABOUT THE AUTHOR

Elle Kennedy grew up in the suburbs of Toronto, Ontario, and holds a B.A. in English from York University. From an early age she knew she wanted to be a writer, and actively began pursuing that dream when she was only a teenager. When she's not writing, she's reading. And when she's not reading, she's making music with her drummer boyfriend, oil painting, or indulging her love for board games. Elle loves to hear from her readers. Visit her at her Web site, www.ellekennedy.com, or stop by her blog, sizzlingpens.blogspot.com, to chat with Elle and her fellow Harlequin writers.

I could not have written this book without my fantastic critique partners, Lori Borrill and Jennifer Lewis, two incredible authors in their own right, and the best support system a girl could have.

I'd also like to dedicate this book to...

My family and friends, for not letting me give up.

Tyler, Amanda and Brad, for all their help with this story.

My fabulous editor Laura Barth. And senior editor Brenda Chin for taking a chance on me and my hockey-playing hero!

1

"I REALLY NEED to get laid," Hayden Houston said with a sigh. She reached for the glass on the smooth mahogany tabletop and took a sip of red wine. The slightly bitter liquid eased her thirst but did nothing to soothe her frustration.

The pictures staring at her from the walls of the Ice House Bar didn't help, either. Action shots of hockey players mid slap shot, framed rookie cards, team photos of the Chicago Warriors—it seemed as if the sport haunted her everywhere she went. Sure, she was a team owner's daughter, but occasionally it would be nice to focus on something other than hockey. Like sex, perhaps.

Across from her, Darcy White grinned. "We haven't seen each other in two years and that's all you've got to say? Come on, Professor, no anecdotes about life in Berkeley? No insightful lectures about Impressionist art?"

"I save the insightful lectures for my students. And as for anecdotes, none of them involve sex so let's not waste time with those."

She ran her hand through her hair and discovered that all the bounce she'd tried to inject into it before heading to the Ice House Bar had deflated. Volume-enhancing mousse? Yeah, right. Apparently nothing could make her stick-straight brown hair look anything other than stick-straight.

"Okay, I'll bite," Darcy said. "Why do you have sex on the brain?"

"Because I'm not getting any."

Darcy sipped her strawberry daiquiri, a drink she'd confessed she hated but drank anyway, claiming men found it sexy. "Aren't you seeing someone back in California? Dan? Drake?"

"Doug," Hayden corrected.

"How long have you been together?"

"Two months."

"And you still haven't done the mattress mambo?"

"Nope."

"You're kidding, right? He's not down with getting it on?" Darcy paused, looking thoughtful. "Or should I say, he's not *up* with it?"

"Oh, he's up. He just wants, and I quote, 'to get to know each other fully before we cross the intimacy bridge.'"

Her friend hooted. "The intimacy bridge? Girl, he sounds like a total loser. Dump him. Now. Before he brings up the intimacy bridge again."

"We're actually on a break right now," Hayden admitted. "Before I left I told him I needed some space."

"Space? Uh-uh. I think what you need is a new boyfriend."

God, that was the last thing she wanted. Toss her line in the dating pool and start fishing again? No, thank you. After three failed relationships in five years, Hayden had decided to quit falling for bad boys and focus on the good ones. And Doug Lloyd was definitely a good one. He taught a Renaissance course at Berkeley, he was intelligent and witty, and he valued love and commitment as much as she did. Having grown up with a single father, Hayden longed for a partner she could build a home and grow old with.

Her mom had died in a car accident when Hayden was a baby, and her dad had given up on finding love again, opting instead to spend more than twenty years focusing on his hockey-coaching career. He'd finally remarried three years ago, but she suspected loneliness, rather than love, had driven him to do so. Why else would he have proposed to a woman after four months of dating? A woman who was twenty-nine years his junior. A woman he was in the process of divorcing, no less.

Well, she had no intention of following her dad's example. She wasn't going to spend decades alone and then jump into marriage with someone totally unsuitable.

Doug held the same mind-set. He was a traditionalist through and through, a believer that marriage should be valued and not rushed into. Besides, he had a rock-hard body that made her mouth water. He'd even let her touch it...once. They'd been kissing on the couch in the living room of her San Francisco town house and she'd slid her hands underneath his button-down shirt. Running her fingers over his rippled chest, she'd murmured, "Let's move this into the bedroom."

That's when he'd dropped the no-intimacy bomb on her. He'd assured her he was unbelievably attracted to her, but that, like marriage, he didn't believe sex should be rushed. He wanted the first time to be special.

And no amount of chest rubbing could persuade him to let go of his chivalrous intentions.

And therein lay the problem. Doug was simply too *nice.* At first she'd thought his views on making love were really very sweet. But two months, coupled with *eight* months of celibacy prior to meeting Doug, added up to extreme sexual frustration on her part.

She loved that Doug was a gentleman but, darn it, sometimes a girl just needed a *man.*

"Seriously, this Damian guy seems like a wimp," Darcy said, jerking her from her thoughts.

"Doug."

"Whatever." Darcy waved a dismissive hand and tossed her

long red hair over her shoulder. "Screw intimacy. If Dustin won't have sex with you, find someone who will."

"Believe me, I'm tempted."

More than tempted, actually. The next couple months were bound to be pure hell. She'd come home after final exams to support her father through his messy divorce, to be the good daughter, but that didn't mean she had to like the situation.

Her stepmother was determined to squeeze Hayden's dad for every dime he had. And, boy, did he have a lot of dimes. Though he'd spent most of his life coaching, Presley had always dreamed of owning a team, a goal he'd finally reached seven years ago. Thanks to the substantial insurance settlement he'd received after her mom's accident, and his wise investment in a pharmaceutical company that had made him millions, he'd been able to purchase the Chicago Warriors franchise. Over the years he'd continued investing and building his fortune, but his main priority was the team. It was all he ever thought about, and that's what made coming home so difficult.

Her childhood had been chaotic, to say the least. Traveling with her dad across the country for away games, living in Florida for two years when he'd coached the Aces to a championship victory, five years in Texas, three in Oregon. It had been tough, but Hayden's close relationship with her dad had made the constant upheaval bearable. Her father had always shown an interest in her life. He'd listened while she babbled about her favorite artists, and taken her to countless museums over the years.

Now that she was an adult and he was busy with the team, he no longer seemed to care about making time to connect with her outside of the hockey arena. She knew other team owners didn't get as involved as her father did, but his background as a coach seemed to influence his new position; he had his hand in every aspect of the Warriors, from drafting players to marketing, and he thrived on it, no matter how time-consuming the work was.

That's why three years ago she'd decided to accept the full-time position Berkeley had offered her, even though it meant relocating to the West Coast. She'd figured the old absence-makes-the-heart-grow-fonder cliché might kick in and make her father realize there was more to life than hockey. It hadn't.

So she'd come back to see him through the divorce in hopes that they could reconnect.

"Have you become a nymphomaniac since you left town?" Darcy was asking. "You never mentioned it in your e-mails."

Hayden forced herself to focus on her best friend and not dwell on her issues with her dad. "I haven't become a nymphomaniac. I'm just stressed-out and I need to unwind. Do you blame me?"

"Not really. The evil stepmother is throwing poison apples all over the place, huh?"

"You saw the morning paper, too?"

"Oh, yeah. Pretty crappy."

Hayden raked her fingers through her hair. "Crappy? It's a disaster."

"Any truth to it?" Darcy asked carefully.

"Of course not! Dad would never do the things she's accusing him of." She tried to control the frustration in her tone. "Let's not talk about this. Tonight I just want to forget about my dad and Sheila and the whole messy business."

"All right. Wanna talk about sex again?"

Hayden grinned. "No. I'd rather *have* sex instead."

"Then do it. There are tons of men in this place. Pick one and go home with him."

"You mean a one-night stand?" she asked warily.

"Hell, yeah."

"I don't know. It seems kind of sleazy, hopping into bed with someone and never seeing them again."

"How is that sleazy? I do it all the time."

Hayden burst out laughing. "Of course you do. You're commitment-phobic."

Darcy went through men like socks, and some of the details she shared in her e-mails made Hayden gape. *She* certainly couldn't remember ever experiencing seven orgasms in one night, or indulging in a ménage à trois with two firefighters she'd met—figure this one out—at an illegal bonfire in Chicago's Lincoln Park.

Darcy raised her eyebrows, blue eyes flashing with challenge. "Well, let me ask you this—what sounds more fun, having a few screaming orgasms with a man you may or may not see again, or hiking across the intimacy bridge with Don?"

"Doug."

Darcy shrugged. "I think we both know my way is better than the highway. Or should I say the bridge?" She fluttered her hand as if waving a white flag. "Sorry, I promise to refrain from any further bridge comments for the rest of the evening."

Hayden didn't answer. Instead, she mulled over Darcy's suggestion. She'd never had a one-night stand in her life. For her, sex came with other things, relationship things, like going to dinner, spending a cozy night in, saying *I love you* for the first time.

But why did sex always have to be about love? Couldn't it just be purely for pleasure? No dinner, no I-love-you's, no expectations?

"I don't know," she said slowly. "Falling into bed with a man when last week I was still with Doug?"

"You asked for space for a reason," Darcy said. "Might as well take advantage of it."

"By going to bed with someone else." She sipped her wine, thoughtful and hesitant at the same time.

"Why not?" Darcy said. "Look, you've spent years searching for a guy to build a life with—maybe you should try looking for one who jump-starts your libido instead. The way I see it, it's time for you to have some fun, Hayden. I think you need fun."

She sighed. "I think so, too."

Darcy's grin widened. "You're seriously considering it, aren't you?"

"If I see a guy I like, I just might."

Her own words surprised her, but they made sense. What was so wrong with hooking up with a stranger in a bar? People did wild things like that all the time, and maybe right now she needed to be a little wild.

Darcy twirled the straw around in her daiquiri glass, looking pensive. "What's your pseudonym going to be?"

"My pseudonym?" she echoed.

"Yeah. If you're going to do this right, you need total anonymity. Be someone else for the night. Like Yolanda."

"No way," she objected with a laugh. "I'd rather just be myself."

"Fine." Darcy's shoulders drooped.

"We're getting ahead of ourselves, Darce. Shouldn't I pick the guy first?"

Darcy's enthusiasm returned. "Good point. Let's spin the man wheel and see who it lands on."

Stifling a laugh, Hayden followed her friend's lead and swept her eyes around the crowded bar. Everywhere she looked, she saw men. Tall ones, short ones, cute ones, bald ones. None of them sparked her interest.

And then she saw him.

Standing at the counter with his back turned to them was

the lucky winner of the man wheel. All she could see was a head of dark brown hair, a broad back clad in a navy-blue sweater and long legs encased in denim. Oh, and the butt. Hard not to notice that tight little butt.

"Excellent selection," Darcy teased, following her gaze.

"I can't see his face," she complained, trying not to crane her neck.

"Patience, grasshopper."

Holding her breath, Hayden watched the man drop a few bills on the sleek mahogany counter and accept a tall glass of beer from the bartender. When he turned around, she sucked in an impressed gasp. The guy had the face of a Greek god, chiseled, rugged, with intense blue eyes that caused her heart to pound and sensual lips that made her mouth tingle. And he was huge. With his back turned he hadn't seemed this big, but now, face-to-face, she realized he stood well over six feet and had the kind of chest a woman wanted to rest her head on. She could see the muscular planes of his chest even through his sweater.

"Wow," she muttered, more to herself than Darcy.

A shiver of anticipation danced through her as she imagined spending the night with him.

Beer in hand, the man strode toward one of the pool tables at the far end of the bar, and headed for the cue rack. Setting his glass on the small ledge along the wall, he grabbed a cue and proceeded to rack the balls on the green felt table. A second later, a tall, lanky college-age kid approached and they exchanged a few words. The kid snatched up a cue and joined Mr. Delicious at the table.

Hayden turned back to Darcy and saw her friend rolling her eyes. "What?" she said, feeling a bit defensive.

"What are you waiting for?" Darcy prompted.

She glanced at the dark-haired sex god again. "I should go over there?"

"If you're serious about doing the nasty tonight, then, yeah, go over there."

"And do what?"

"Shoot some pool. Talk. Flirt. You know, look under the hood before you commit to buying the car."

"He's not a car, Darce."

"Yeah, but if he was, he'd be something dangerously hot, like a Hummer."

Hayden burst out laughing. If there was one thing to be said about Darcy, it was that she truly was one of a kind.

"Come on, go over there," Darcy repeated.

She swallowed. "Now?"

"No, next week."

Her mouth grew even drier, prompting her to down the rest of her wine.

"You're seriously nervous about this, aren't you?" Darcy said, blue eyes widening in wonder. "When did you become so shy? You give lectures to classes of hundreds. He's just one man, Hayden."

Her eyes drifted back in the guy's direction. She noticed how his back muscles bunched together as he rested his elbows on the pool table, how his taut backside looked practically edible in those faded jeans.

He's just one man, she said to herself, shaking off her nerves. Right. Just one tall, sexy, oozing-with-raw-masculinity man.

This would be a piece of cake.

BRODY CROFT CIRCLED the pool table, his eyes sharp as a hawk's as he examined his options. With a quick nod, he pointed and said, "Thirteen, side pocket."

His young companion, wearing a bright red Hawaiian T-shirt that made Brody's eyes hurt, raised his eyebrows. "Really? Tough shot, man."

"I can handle it."

And handle it he did. The ball slid cleanly into the pocket, making the kid beside him groan.

"Nice, man. Nice."

"Thanks." He moved to line up his next shot when he noticed his opponent staring at him. "Something wrong?"

"No, uh, nothing's wrong. Are—are you Brody Croft?" the guy blurted out, looking embarrassed.

Brody smothered a laugh. He'd wondered how long it would take the kid to ask. Not that he was conceited enough to think everyone on the planet knew who he was, but seeing as this bar was owned by Alexi Nicklaus and Jeff Wolinski, two fellow Warriors, most of the patrons were bound to be hockey fans.

"At your service," he said easily, extending his hand.

The kid gripped it tightly, as if he were sinking in a pit of quicksand and Brody's hand was the lifeline keeping him alive. "This is so awesome! I'm Mike, by the way."

The look of pure adoration on Mike's face brought a knot of discomfort to Brody's gut. He always enjoyed meeting fans, but sometimes the hero worship went a little too far.

"What do you say we keep playing?" he suggested, gesturing to the pool table.

"Yeah. I mean, sure! Let's play!" Mike's eyes practically popped out of his angular face. "I can't wait to tell the guys I played a round of pool with Brody Croft."

Since he couldn't come up with a response that didn't include something asinine, like "thank you," Brody chalked up the end of his cue. The next shot would be more difficult than the first, but again, nothing he couldn't manage. He'd worked in a bar like this one back when he'd played for the farm team and was barely bringing in enough cash to feed his goldfish, let alone himself. He used to hang out after work shooting pool with the other waiters, eventually developing a fondness for the game. With the way his schedule was now, he rarely had time to play anymore.

But with rumors about a possible league investigation swirling, thanks to allegations made in a recent interview with the team owner's soon-to-be ex-wife, Brody might end up with more free time than he wanted. Mrs. Houston apparently had proof that her husband had bribed at least two players to bring forth a loss and that he'd placed substantial—*illegal*—bets on those fixed games.

While there was probably no truth to any of it, Brody was growing concerned with the rumors.

A few years ago a similar scandal had plagued the Colorado Kodiaks. Only three players had been involved, but many innocent players suffered—other teams were reluctant to pick them up due to their association with the tarnished franchise.

Hell would freeze over before he'd accept a payout, and he had no intention of being lumped in with any of the players who might have. His contract was due to expire at the end of the season. He'd be a free agent then, which meant he needed to remain squeaky clean if he wanted to sign with a new team or remain with the Warriors.

He tried to remind himself that this morning's paper was filled with nothing but rumors. If something materialized from Sheila Houston's claims, he'd worry about it then. Right now, he needed to focus on playing his best so the Warriors could win the first play-offs round and move on to the next.

Resting the cue between his thumb and forefinger, Brody positioned the shot, took one last look and pulled the cue back.

From the corner of his eye, a woman's curvy figure drew his attention, distracting him just as he pushed the cue forward. The brief diversion caused his fingers to slip, and the white ball sailed across the felt, avoided every other ball on the table and slid directly into the far pocket. Scratch.

Damn.

Scowling, he lifted his head just as the source of his distraction drew near.

"You could do it over," Mike said quickly, fumbling for the white ball and placing it back on the table. "It's called a mulligan or something."

"That's golf," Brody muttered, his gaze glued to the approaching brunette.

A few years ago an interviewer for *Sports Illustrated* had asked him to describe the type of women he was attracted to. "Leggy blondes" had been his swift response, which was pretty much the exact opposite of the woman who'd now stopped two feet in front of him. And yet his mouth went dry at the sight of her, his body quickly responding to every little detail. The silky chocolate-brown hair falling over her shoulders, the vibrant green eyes the same shade as a lush rain forest, the petite body with more curves than his brain could register.

His breath hitched as their eyes met. The whisper of an uncertain smile that tugged at her full lips sent a jolt to his groin. Jeez. He couldn't remember the last time a single smile from a woman had evoked such an intense response.

"I thought I'd play the winner." Her soft, husky voice promptly delivered another shock wave to Brody's crotch.

Stunned to find he was two seconds away from a full-blown erection, he tried to remind his body that he wasn't a teenager any longer, but a twenty-nine-year-old man who knew how to control himself. Hell, he could control the puck while fending off elbows and cross-checks from opposing attackers; getting a hold of his hormones should be a piece of cake.

"Here, just take my place now," Mike burst out, quickly pushing his cue into her hands. His gaze dropped to the cleavage spilling over the scooped neckline of the brunette's yellow tank top, and then the kid turned to Brody and winked. "Have fun, man."

Brody wrinkled his brow, wondering if Mike thought he was graciously passing this curvy bombshell over to him or something, but before he could say anything, Mike disappeared in the crowd.

Brody swallowed, then focused his eyes on the sexy little woman who'd managed to get him hard with one smile.

She didn't look like the type you'd find in a sports bar, even one as upscale as this. Sure, her body was out of this world, but something about her screamed innocence. The freckles splattering the bridge of her nose maybe, or perhaps the way she kept biting on the corner of her bottom lip like a bunny nibbling on a piece of lettuce.

Before he could stop it, the image of those plump red lips nibbling on one particular part of his anatomy slid to the forefront of his brain like a well-placed slap shot to the net. His cock pushed against the fly of his jeans.

So much for controlling his hormones.

"I'm guessing it's my turn," she said. Tilting her head, she offered another endearing smile. "Seeing as you just blew your shot."

He cleared his throat. "Uh, yeah."

Snap out of it, man.

Right, he needed to regroup here. He played hockey, yeah, but he wasn't a player anymore. His love-'em-and-leave-'em ways were in the past. He was sick to death of women fawning all over him because of his career. Nowadays all he had to do was walk into a place—club, bar, the public library—and a warm, willing female was by his side, ready to jump his bones. And he couldn't even count the number of times he'd heard, "Do you like it rough off the ice, baby?"

Well, screw it. He'd been down the casual road, had his fun, scored off the ice as often as he scored on it, but now it was time to take a new path. One where the woman in his bed actually gave a damn about *him,* and not the hockey star she couldn't wait to gush to her friends about.

The sexual fog in his brain cleared, leaving him alert and composed, and completely aware of the flush on the brunette's cheeks and the hint of attraction in her eyes. If this woman was looking to score with Mr. Hockey, she had another think coming.

"I'm Hayden," his new opponent said, uncertainty floating through her forest-green eyes.

"Brody Croft," he returned coolly, waiting for the flicker of recognition to cross her features.

It didn't happen. No flash of familiarity, no widening of the eyes. Her expression didn't change in the slightest.

"It's nice to meet you. Brody." Her voice lingered on his name, as if she were testing it out for size. She must have decided she liked the fit, because she gave a small nod and turned her attention to the table. After a quick examination, she pointed to the ball he'd failed to sink and called the shot.

Okay, was he supposed to believe she genuinely didn't know who he was? That she'd walked into a sports bar and randomly chosen to hit on the only hockey player in attendance?

"So…did you catch the game last night?" he said with a casual slant of the head.

She gave him a blank stare. "What game?"

"Game one of the play-offs, Warriors and Vipers. Seriously good hockey, in my opinion."

Her brows drew together in a frown. "Oh. I'm not really a fan, to be honest."

"You don't like the Warriors?"

"I don't like hockey." She made a self-deprecating face.

"Actually, I can't say I enjoy any sport, really. Maybe the gymnastics in the summer Olympics?"

He couldn't help but grin. "Are you asking or telling?"

She smiled back. "Telling. And I guess it's very telling that I only watch a sports event once every four years, huh?"

He found himself liking the dry note to her throaty voice when she admitted her disinterest in sports. Her honesty was rare. Most—fine, *all*—of the women he encountered claimed to love his sport of choice, and if they didn't truly love it, they pretended to, as if sharing that common interest made them soul mates.

"But I love this game," Hayden added, raising her cue. "It counts as a sport, right?"

"It does in my book."

She nodded, then focused on the balls littering the table. She leaned forward to take her shot.

He got a nice eyeful of her cleavage, a tantalizing swell of creamy-white skin spilling over the neckline of her snug yellow top. When he lowered his eyes, he couldn't help but admire her full breasts, hugged firmly by a thin bra he could only see the outline of.

She took the shot, and he raised his brows, impressed, as the ball cleanly disappeared into the pocket. She was good.

All right, more than good, he had to relent as she proceeded to circle the table and sink ball after ball.

"Where'd you learn to play like that?" he asked, finally finding his voice.

She met his eyes briefly before sinking the last solid on the table. "My dad." She smiled again. Those pouty lips just screamed for his mouth to do wicked things to them. "He bought me my own table when I was nine, set it up right next to his. We used to play side by side in the basement every night before I went to bed."

"Does he still play?"

Her eyes clouded. "No. He's too busy with work to relax around a pool table anymore." She straightened her back and glanced at the table. "Eight ball, corner pocket."

At this point, Brody didn't even care about the game Hayden was certain to win. The sweet scent of her perfume, a fruity sensual aroma, floated in the air and made him mindless with need. Man, he couldn't remember the last time he'd been so drawn to a woman.

After sinking the eight ball, she moved toward him, each step she took heightening his desire. She ran her fingers through her dark hair, and a new aroma filled his nostrils. Strawberries. Coconut.

He was suddenly very, very hungry.

"Good game," she said, shooting him another smile. Impish, this time.

His mouth twisted wryly. "I didn't even get to play."

"I'm sorry." She paused. "Do you like to play?"

Was she referring to pool? Or a different game? Maybe the kind you played in bed. Naked.

"Pool, I mean," she added quickly.

"Sure, I like pool. Among other things." *Let's see how she handles that.*

A cute rosy flush spread over her cheeks. "Me, too. I mean, I like other things."

His curiosity sparked as he stared at the enigma in front of him. He got the distinct impression that she was flirting with him. Or trying to, at least. Yet her unmistakable blush and the slight trembling of her hands betrayed the confident air she tried to convey.

Did she do this often? Flirt with strange men in bars? Looking at her again, now that he was able to see through the fog of initial attraction, it didn't seem like the case. She was dressed rather conservatively. Sure, the top was low-cut, but it covered her midriff, and her jeans didn't ride low on her hips like those of most of the other women in this place. And sexy as she was, she didn't seem to be aware of her own appeal.

"That's good. Other things can be a lot of fun," he answered, unable to stop the husky pitch of his voice.

Their gazes connected. Brody could swear the air crackled and hissed with sexual tension. Or maybe he just imagined it. He couldn't deny the hum of awareness thudding in his groin like the bass line of a sultry jazz tune, but maybe he was alone in the feeling. It was difficult to get a read on Hayden.

"So…Brody." His name rolled off her lips in a way that had his body growing stiff. That didn't say much, considering that every part of him was already hard and prickling with anticipation.

He wanted her in his bed.

Whoa—where had that come from?

Five minutes ago he was telling himself it was time to quit falling into bed with women who didn't give a damn about him and look for something more meaningful. So why the hell was he anticipating a roll in the hay with a woman he'd just met?

Because she's different.

The observation came out of nowhere, bringing with it a baffling swirl of emotion. Yes, this woman had somehow managed to elicit primal, greedy lust in him. Yes, her body was designed to drive a man wild. But something about her seriously intrigued him. Those damn cute freckles, the shy smiles, the look in her eyes that clearly said, "I want to go to bed with you but I'm apprehensive about it." It was the combination of sensuality and bashfulness, excitement and wariness, that attracted him to her.

He opened his mouth to say something, anything, but promptly closed it when Hayden reached out to touch his arm.

Looking up at him with those bottomless green eyes, she said, "Look, I know this is going to sound…forward. And don't think I do this often—I've never done this actually, but…" She took a breath. "Would you like to come back to my hotel?"

Ah, her hotel. An out-of-towner. That explained why she hadn't recognized him. And yet he got the feeling that even if she did know what he did for a living, she wouldn't care.

He liked that.

"Well?" she said, fixing him with an expectant stare.

He couldn't stop the teasing twinge in his voice. "And what will we do in your hotel room?"

A hint of a smile. "We could have a nightcap."

"A nightcap," he repeated.

"Or we could talk. Watch television. Order room service."

The little vixen was teasing him, he realized. And, damn, but he liked this side of her, too.

"Maybe raid the minifridge?"

"Definitely."

Their eyes met and locked, the heat of desire and promise of sex filling the space between them. Finally he shoved his pool cue in the rack and strode back to her. Screw it. He'd told himself no more sleazy bar pickups, but damn it, this didn't feel sleazy. It felt *right*.

Barely able to disguise the urgency in his tone, he curled his fingers over her hot, silky skin and said, "Let's go."

2

DEAR GOD, he'd said yes.

She'd invited a gorgeous stranger back to her hotel room for a *nightcap* (translation: sex) and he'd actually said *yes*.

Hayden resisted the urge to fan her hot face with her hands. Instead, trying to remain cool and collected, she said, "I'll meet you outside, okay? I just need to tell my friend I'm leaving."

His smoldering blue eyes studied her for a moment, making her grow hotter. With a quick nod, he exited the bar. Tearing her attention away from his criminally sexy backside, she spun on her heel and hurried back to Darcy, dodging people along the way. When she reached the table, Darcy greeted her with a delighted grin. "You bad girl, you," she teased, wagging her finger.

Sliding into the chair, Hayden swallowed hard and willed her heartbeat to slow. "Jesus. I can't believe I'm doing this."

"I take it he said yes?"

Hayden ignored the question. "I just propositioned a complete stranger. Granted, he's a very sexy stranger, but hell! I'm not sure I can do this."

"Of course you can."

"But I don't even know him. What if he hacks me to pieces and hides my dismembered body parts in the air-conditioning system of the hotel or something?"

"You have your cell phone?"

She nodded.

"If you see any sign of trouble, call the cops. Or call me and I'll call the cops." Darcy shrugged. "But I wouldn't worry. He doesn't seem like the serial-killer type."

Hayden blew out a breath. "That's what they said about Ted Bundy."

"You can back out, you know. You don't have to sleep with this guy. But you want to, don't you?"

Did she want to? Oh, yeah. As the image of Brody's chiseled face and scrumptious body flashed through her brain, some of her nervousness dissolved. He was hands down the most gorgeous man she'd ever met. And she got the feeling he knew his way around a bedroom. The raw sex appeal pouring out of him told her she might be in for a very stimulating night.

"I want to." Newfound confidence washed over her. "And I probably shouldn't keep him waiting."

Darcy winked. "Have fun."

"Are you going to be okay here alone?"

"Of course." Darcy gestured to her fruity pink drink. "This daiquiri will attract the fellows like flies to honey. For the purpose of this analogy, I'll be the honey."

Hayden laughed. "Whatever you say."

With a quick wave, she threaded through the crowd toward the door. When she stepped into the cool night air, she spotted Brody standing near one of the potted plants in the entrance, his hands slung in the pockets of his jeans. A shiver tickled her belly as she took in his profile. He really was spectacular. Her gaze lowered to his lips. She wondered what they would feel like pressed against her own. Would they be soft? Hard? Both?

"Hey," she said, her voice wavering.

She took a step forward just as he turned to face her. His expression, appreciative, anticipatory, sizzled her nerves. "Your car or mine?" he asked in a rough voice that made her toes curl.

"I don't have a car. My friend drove here." A squeak, her voice had come out in a damn squeak.

"My car's over there." He nodded, then began walking toward the parking lot. He didn't check to see if she was following. As if he just assumed she was.

This was her chance to walk away. She could hurry into the bar and pretend she'd never asked this man to come back to her hotel. She could phone up Doug, have a heart-to-heart, maybe entice him into engaging in some phone sex…. Ha! Fat chance.

She hurried to keep up with Brody's purposeful strides.

"Nice car," she remarked when they reached the shiny black BMW SUV.

"Thanks." He pulled a set of keys from his front pocket and pressed a button. The car's security system beeped as the doors unlocked, and he reached for the passenger door and opened it for her. Hayden settled against the leather seat and waited for Brody to get in.

After he'd buckled his seat belt and started the engine, he turned to her and asked, "Where to?"

"The Ritz-Carlton."

He raised his eyebrows but didn't say anything, just pulled out of the parking lot and made a left turn. "So where are you from, Hayden?"

"I was born in Chicago, but I've been living in San Francisco for the past three years."

"And what do you do out there?"

"I'm a junior professor at Berkeley. I teach art history, and I'm also working toward a Ph.D."

Before she could ask him what he did for a living, he said, "Sounds exciting."

She got the feeling he wasn't talking about her career

anymore. Her suspicions were confirmed when his gaze swept over face and dropped to her cleavage. Under his brief—but appreciative—scrutiny, her nipples tightened against her lace bra.

She played with the sleeve of the green wool sweater she'd brought instead of a coat, focusing on the scenery along South Michigan Avenue, afraid to look at him again. If he got her this aroused from one hooded glance, what on earth would he do to her in bed?

Gosh, she couldn't wait to find out.

The rest of the car ride was silent. They reached the hotel, and Brody pulled into the lot and killed the engine. Still, neither of them spoke. As she unbuckled her seat belt, her pulse began to race. This was it. An hour ago she'd been complaining to Darcy about the lack of sex in her life, and now here she was, walking into the lobby of the Ritz with the sexiest man she'd ever encountered.

Her heart thumped against her rib cage as they rode the elevator up to the penthouse. Shooting her a quizzical look, he said, "You must make good money at Berkeley."

She simply nodded, her expression vague. She didn't want to tell him that the lavish penthouse actually belonged to her father. Her dad had lived here up until three years ago, before he'd married Sheila. He kept the place so Hayden would have somewhere to stay when she came to visit. But she didn't want to tell Brody, mostly because that would lead to questions like *what does your father do?* Which would then lead to questions about her dad's hockey team and that was one topic of conversation she tried to avoid.

With the exception of Doug, most of the men she'd dated over the years had gone a little crazy when they found out her father owned the Warriors. Once, she'd dated a man who'd badgered her constantly to get him season tickets—which had driven her to promptly break up with him.

She understood the sports obsession that came with most males, but just once it would be nice if *she* were the source of a man's infatuation.

The elevator doors opened right into the living room. Decorated in shades of black and gold, the room boasted four enormous leather couches in the center, all positioned in the direction of a fifty-six-inch plasma television mounted on the far wall. The suite had three large bedrooms, as well as a private covered balcony with a ten-person hot tub. In the corner of the main suite was a wet bar, which Hayden made a beeline for the second they stepped inside.

She wasn't a big drinker, but her nerves were shaky, making her hands tremble and her heartbeat erratic, and she hoped the alcohol might calm her down.

"What can I get you?" she called over her shoulder. "There's beer, scotch, whiskey, bourbon—"

"You." With a soft laugh, Brody eliminated the distance between them.

Oh, God, he was huge. She had to fully tilt her head up to look at him. At five feet three inches, she felt like a dwarf next to him. Her heart jammed in her throat as he stepped even closer. She could feel his body heat, his warm breath tickling her ear as he leaned down and whispered, "That was the nightcap you were referring to, wasn't it?"

His low, husky voice heated her veins. When she met his eyes, she saw the unmistakable desire glittering in their cobalt-blue depths. "Well?" he prompted.

"Yes." The word squeaked out of her mouth.

He settled his big hands on her waist, yet didn't press his body against hers. Despite the pounding of her heart, anticipation began to build in her belly, slowly crept up to her breasts like a vine and made them grow heavy, achy. She wanted him closer, wanted to feel his firm chest on her breasts, his hardness between her thighs.

Brody lifted one hand and brushed his thumb against her lower lip. "If you want to change your mind, now's the time."

He waited for her answer, watching her closely. Her throat grew dry, while another part of her grew wet.

Did she want to change her mind? Maybe she should call her own bluff now, before things got out of hand. But as she studied his handsome face, she realized she didn't want him to leave. So what if this wouldn't result in I-love-you's and cosigning a mortgage for a house? Tonight wasn't about that. Tonight she was stressed and tired and sexually frustrated. And just once she wanted to be with a man without thinking about the future.

"I haven't changed my mind," she murmured.

"Good."

He skimmed his hand over her hip, moving it to her back, grazing her tailbone. Then he stared at her lips, as if pondering, debating.

His slow perusal lasted too long for her throbbing body. She wanted him to kiss her. Now. She let out a tiny groan to voice her anguish.

Amusement danced across his features. "What? What do you want, Hayden?"

"Your mouth." The words flew out before she could stop them, shocking her. Since when was she this forward?

"All right." He dipped his head and planted a soft kiss on her neck, lightly biting the tender flesh with his teeth.

She whimpered and he responded with a chuckle, his warm breath moistening her skin. He trailed his tongue up to her earlobe, flicked over it, licked it, then blew a stream of air over it, making her shiver.

Fire began simmering in her blood, heating all the parts that already ached for him. She reached up and touched his dark hair, relishing the silky texture. She'd never known a simple kiss could have such a slow buildup. Most of the men in her past had thrust their tongues into her mouth and quickly followed suit by thrusting themselves into her.

But Brody, he took his time.

He tortured her.

"Your skin tastes like…" He kissed her jaw, then nipped at it. "Strawberries. And honey."

All she could do was shiver in response.

"Take off your clothes," he said roughly.

She swallowed. "Now?"

"Now would be a good time, yes."

She reached for the hem of her sweater, trying to fight the insecurity spiraling through her. She'd never stripped for a man before. Was she supposed to put on a show? Dance? Well, forget that. No matter how much she wanted him right now, she wasn't going to pretend to be the sexy seductress she wasn't.

She pulled her sweater and tank top over her head, pleased to hear Brody's breath hitch at the sight of her lacy wisp of a bra. When she reached for the front clasp, he shook his head. "No. Not yet. First the jeans."

Well. Commanding, wasn't he?

Obligingly, she wiggled out of her jeans and let them drop to the floor. Her black panties matched her bra, and they, too, left little to the imagination.

Brody's eyes widened with approval. She was starting to get the hang of this stripping thing. Hooking her thumbs under the spaghetti-thin straps that constituted a waistband, she pulled her panties down her thighs, slowly, bending over a little so he could get a peek at her cleavage.

Naked from the waist down, she held his gaze. "Like what you see?"

His serious expression never faltered. "Very much. Now the bra."

In one slow, fluid movement, she unclasped her bra and tossed it aside. Strangely enough, she no longer felt insecure.

"I like—" he stepped closer and brushed his thumb over the swell of one breast "—these. A lot."

She wondered if he realized he still hadn't kissed her lips. Though the way his eyes burned every inch of skin she'd just exposed to him, she felt thoroughly kissed.

"Your turn. Get rid of your clothes."

He grinned. "Why don't you do it for me?"

The thought of undressing him was so appealing that her nipples hardened. He didn't miss the reaction, and his grin widened.

"Gets you going, doesn't it, the thought of peeling these clothes off my body?" he taunted.

"Yes," she blew out.

"Then do it."

With a shaky breath, she grasped his sweater, bunching the material between her fingers before lifting it up his chest and over his head. That first sight of his bare chest stole the breath from her lungs. Every inch of him was hard. His defined pectorals, the rippling abs and trim hips. He had a two-inch scar under his collarbone, and another under his chin that she hadn't noticed before, but the scars only added to his appeal, making him appear dangerous.

A badass tribal tattoo covered one firm bicep, while the other boasted a lethal-looking dragon in mid-flight. It reminded her of her own tattoo, the one she'd gotten for the sole purpose of pissing off her father after he'd grounded her for missing curfew when she was seventeen. Even now the spontaneity of her actions—getting a *tattoo!*—surprised her.

Darcy always teased that she had a secret wild side, and maybe she did, but it rarely made any appearances.

Tonight, though, her wild side had definitely come out to play.

"Like what you see?" Brody mimicked, the heat in his eyes telling her he was enjoying the attention.

She licked her lips. "Yes." Then she reached for his fly, unbuttoned it and pulled the zipper down. She bent over to slide his jeans off, admiring his long legs and muscular thighs and the erection that pushed against the black boxer briefs he wore, a thick ridge that made her mouth water.

Dear God, this was insanity.

Stumbling to her feet, she tugged at his waistband and helped him out of the briefs. Leaving him as naked as she was.

She shyly appraised his body, which was toned, muscled and unbelievably *male*. She eyed his impressive erection, then trembled at the thought of that hard, pulsing cock buried deep inside her.

Suddenly she could no longer bear it.

"For God's sake, kiss me," she blurted out.

"Yes, ma'am." His eyes gleaming, Brody pressed his body against hers and finally bent down to capture her mouth.

Oh, sweet Jesus.

He felt and tasted like heaven. With skilled ease, he explored her mouth, swirling and thrusting his tongue into every crevice, hot and greedy. When he sucked on her bottom lip, she let out a deep moan then pulled back and stared at him in awe.

Brody seemed to know exactly what to do, turning her on in a way she'd never anticipated. He fondled her breasts for an excruciatingly long time before finally dipping his head and sampling one mound with his tongue.

He sucked the nipple hard, flicked his tongue over it,

nibbled on it until she cried out with pleasure that bordered on pain, and just when she thought it couldn't possibly feel better than that, he turned his attention to her other breast.

Arousal drummed through her body, until her thighs grew slick from her own wetness, and she found herself choking out, "We need a bed. Now."

DAMN, HE HADN'T expected her to be like this. Deliciously demanding and so gorgeous. Something about Hayden sent lust and curiosity spinning through him, the need to both claim her and unravel the mystery of her.

And there was definitely plenty to learn about this freckle-faced professor who had initiated a one-night stand when it was obviously not in her nature.

He sucked on her nipple once more before pulling his head away and straightening his back. His mouth went dry as sawdust as he stared at the evidence of his handiwork on those high, full breasts. His stubble had chafed the hell out of her creamy white skin, leaving splotches of red, and the tips of her dusky pink nipples glistened with the moisture, making him want to feast on her again.

His eyes dropped to the wispy line of dark hair between her thighs. He knew it was called a landing strip and goddamn but he couldn't wait to land his tongue down there. The sparse amount of hair offered a mouthwatering view of her swollen clit.

His already hot and hard body grew hotter and harder.

"Where's the bedroom?" he groaned.

Hayden's mouth quirked. Without answering, she turned on her heel toward the unlit hallway.

Brody took two steps, then stopped when he noticed the tattoo on her lower back. Oh, man. In the shadowy corridor he could just make out the shape of a bird. A hawk, or an eagle. Dark, dangerous, incredibly sexy and completely surprising. He'd known this woman was different. Her tattoo was so tantalizing he marched up to her and gripped her slender waist with both hands.

The top of her head barely reached his chin. How had this saucy little woman reduced him to a state of foolish hunger?

As his hands trailed down her hips, she twisted her head slightly to send him a look that said she was curious about his next move.

His next move consisted of dropping to his knees and outlining the tattoo with his tongue.

Hayden shuddered, but he kept one hand on her waist, keeping her steady. "Why an eagle?" he murmured, kissing her lower back.

"I like eagles."

A very simple answer from a very complicated woman. He stroked her ass with his hand, then lowered his head and bit into the soft flesh.

"Bedroom," she gasped.

"Screw it," he muttered.

Still holding her secure with one hand, he slid the other around to her front and ran one finger over her clit. She hissed out a breath, then jerked forward, pressing her palms to the wall and raising that firm ass so that he got a very naughty view of her glistening sex.

He moved closer as if being pulled by a magnet. As his pulse drummed in his ears, he licked her damp folds from behind and used his finger to stroke her clit.

Hayden shuddered again. "That feels…" she moaned "…amazing."

"What about this? How does this feel?"

He shoved his tongue directly into her opening.

Her breath hitched.

He chuckled at her reaction, then thrust his tongue right back inside her enticing sex before she could catch her breath.

Hayden's soft moans filled the wide hallway. Her breathing grew ragged, her clit swollen beneath his thumb, her sex wet with arousal. He kissed her once more, then moved his mouth away and replaced it with two fingers.

"Are you trying to make me come?" she choked out.

"That was the plan, yeah."

He explored her silky heat, fingering her deftly, enjoying her soft whimpers of pleasure while at the same time trying to ignore his erection, which was threatening to explode.

Any second now his control would shatter, he knew it would, but he held on to that one tiny thread of restraint, feeling it slowly unravel and fray inside him. Hayden's cry of abandon made him move faster, increase his pressure over her clit and add another finger into the mix. And then she came. Loudly. Without inhibition. She pushed her ass into his hand as her inner muscles tightened and contracted over his fingers.

"Oh, God…Brody…" Her voice dissolved into a contented sigh.

A moment later she slid down to the carpeted floor, her bare back pressing into his chest as he continued to trace lazy figure-eights over her clit.

She shifted so they were face-to-face, her green eyes burning with need, her face flushed from her climax. She looked so good that he leaned forward to push his tongue through her pliant lips, intent on exploring every recess of her hot, wet mouth, desperate to taste every part of this woman.

Without breaking the kiss, he rolled her gently onto her back and covered her body with his.

"I need to be inside you," he choked out.

It was a primal urge, an overwhelming desire to possess

and one he never knew he had, but sure enough it was there, making his entire body tense with need, waiting to be released.

Tearing his mouth from hers, he stood up and left her in the hall. He returned a moment later with the condoms that had been tucked in his wallet. Only three condoms, he realized as he glanced down at his hand. Maybe he was being overly optimistic, but as he looked at Hayden, he suspected he might need to make a trip to the drugstore. She hadn't bothered getting up and she looked ridiculously sexy lying there on the floor beneath him. Sexy and trashy and so damn appealing his cock twitched with impatience.

The air was thick with tension, the hallway quiet save for their heavy breathing. Before he could tear open the condom packet, she sat up and murmured, "Not yet."

Then she wrapped her lips around him.

"Jesus," he mumbled, nearly keeling over backward.

The feel of her eager mouth surrounding him brought on an unexpected shudder. She took him deeper into her mouth, cupping his balls, stroking his ass and licking every hard inch of him.

A few moments of exquisite torture were all he could bear. Hard as it was to pull back from the best blow job of his life, he gently moved her head, so close to exploding he wasn't sure how he managed to hold back.

He lowered himself onto her again and Hayden sighed as one palm closed over her breast. "It's been so long…"

"How long?" he asked.

"Too long."

He lightly pinched her nipple before bending down to kiss it. "I'll take it slow then." He sucked the nipple deep in his mouth, rolled the other one between his thumb and forefinger.

She forced his head up and kissed him. "No." She took his hand and dragged it between her legs. "I want fast."

He swallowed when he touched her sex, still moist from her climax.

He grew even harder, wanting so badly to put the damn condom on and slide into her slick heat. But the gentleman in him argued to go slow, to taste every inch of her body and bring her over the edge again before he took his own release. Once more he tried to slow the pace, stroking her with his thumb.

His gentlemanly intentions got him nowhere.

"I'm ready," she said between gritted teeth. "I don't need slow. I need you to fuck me, Brody."

His cock jerked at the wicked request.

Oh, man. He'd never have pegged this woman as a dirty talker. But, damn, how he liked it.

Without another word, he rolled the condom onto his shaft, positioned himself between her thighs and drove deep inside her. They released simultaneous groans.

Burying his face in the curve of her neck, Brody inhaled the sweet feminine scent of her and withdrew, slowly, torturously, only to thrust into her to the hilt before she could blink.

"You're so tight," he muttered in her ear. "So wet."

"Told you I was ready," she said between gasps of pleasure.

He slammed into her, over and over again, groaning each time she lifted her hips to take him deeper. It was too fast for him, and yet it felt like everything was moving in slow motion. The way she dug her fingers into his buttocks and pulled him toward her, squeezing his cock with her tight wetness. The rising pleasure in his body, the impatient throb in his groin that forced him to move even faster.

She exploded again, quivering, shuddering, making little mewling sounds that had his entire body burning with excitement.

He continued plunging into her until finally he couldn't take it anymore. He came a second later, kissing her harshly as his climax rocked into him with the force of a hurricane. Shards of pleasure ripped through him, hot, intense, insistent. Uncontrollable. He fought for air, wondering how it was possible that the little woman beneath him had managed to bring him to the most incredible release of his life.

They lay there for a moment, breathing ragged, bodies slick, his cock still buried inside her.

Hayden ran her hands along his sweat-soaked back, then murmured, "Not bad."

Even in his state of orgasmic numbness Brody managed a mock frown. "Not bad? That's all you can say?"

"Fine, it was tremendously good."

"That's better."

With a small grin, she disentangled herself from his embrace and got to her feet. Her gaze ruefully drifted in the direction of the bedroom they'd never managed to reach. "Five more steps and we could've been on my big, comfortable bed."

He propped himself up on his elbows, the soft carpet itching the hell out of his back. "Don't you worry, Hayden," he said with a rakish glint in his eye. "The night is still young."

3

"HOW MANY?" Darcy demanded the next day.

Hayden moved her cell phone to her other ear and maneuvered her rental car through afternoon traffic. Chicago's downtown core was surprisingly busy; tonight's Warriors game had probably compelled more than a few people to leave work early. Hayden, on the other hand, didn't have a choice in the matter. Whether she wanted to or not, she was about to spend the evening sitting next to her dad in the owner's box, watching a sport she not only found dismally boring, but one she'd resented for years.

God, she couldn't even count how many games she'd been dragged to over the years. Hundreds? Thousands? Regardless of the final tally, she was no closer to liking hockey now, at twenty-six, than she had been at age six, when her father took her to her first game. To her, hockey meant constant uprooting. Traveling, moving, sitting behind the bench with a coloring book because her dad hadn't felt right hiring a nanny.

A shrink would probably tell her that she was projecting, taking out her frustration with her father on an innocent little sport, but she couldn't help it. No matter how hard she'd tried over the years, she couldn't bring herself to appreciate or enjoy the damn game.

"I don't kiss and tell," she said into her cell, stopping at a red light. An El train whizzed overhead, momentarily making her deaf to anything but the thundering of the train as it tore down the tracks.

"Like hell you don't," Darcy was saying when the noise died down. "How many, Hayden?"

Suppressing a tiny smile, she finally caved in. "Five."

"Five!" Darcy went silent for a moment. Then she offered an awe-laced obscenity. "You're telling me the hunk gave you *five orgasms* last night?"

"He sure did." The memory alone brought a spark of heat to her still-exhausted body. Muscles she hadn't even known she had were still aching, thanks to the man who could definitely give the Energizer Bunny a run for its money.

"I'm stunned. You realize that? I'm utterly stunned."

The light ahead turned green and Hayden drove through the intersection. A group of teenagers wearing blue and silver Warriors jerseys caught her attention, and she groaned at the sight of them. She was so not in the mood to watch a night of rowdy hockey with her father.

"So how was the big goodbye and 'thanks for the five O's'?" Darcy asked.

"Strange." She made a left turn and drove down Lakeshore Drive toward the Lincoln Center, the brand-new arena recently built for the Warriors. "Before he left, he asked for my number."

"Did you give it to him?"

"No." She sighed. "But then he offered me *his* number, so I took it."

"It was supposed to be a one-night stand!"

"Yeah…but…he looked so dismayed. I made it pretty clear that it was a one-night thing. You'd think he'd be thrilled about that. No strings, no expectations. But he was disappointed."

"You can't see him again. What if things get serious? You'll be going back to the West Coast in a couple months."

Darcy sounded surprisingly upset. Well, maybe it wasn't that surprising, seeing as Darcy found the idea of falling in love more petrifying than the Ebola virus. The phobia had taken form a few years ago, after Darcy's father broke up his marriage of twenty years by falling in love with another woman. Since then Darcy had convinced herself the same would happen to her. Hayden had tried to assure her friend that not all men left their wives, but her words always fell on deaf ears.

"Nothing will get serious," Hayden said with a laugh. "First of all, I probably won't see Brody again. And second, I won't allow myself to develop a relationship with any man until I figure out where things stand with Doug."

Darcy groaned. "Him? Why do you continue to keep him in the picture? Turn your break into a breakup, before he mentions the intimacy bridge and—"

"Goodbye, Darce."

She hung up, not in the mood to hear Darcy make fun of Doug again. Fine, so he was conservative, and maybe his comparison of sex to a bridge was bizarre, but Doug was a decent man. And she wasn't ready to write him off completely.

Uh, you slept with another man, her conscience reminded.

Her cheeks grew hot at the memory of sleeping with Brody. And somehow the words *sleeping with Brody* seemed unsuitable, as if they described a bland, mundane event like tea with a grandparent. What she and Brody had done last night was neither bland nor mundane. It had been crazy. Intense. Mind-numbingly wild and deliciously dirty. Hands down, the best sex of her life.

Was she a complete fool for sending him away this morning? Probably.

Fine, more like absolutely.

But what else should she have done? She'd woken up to find Brody's smoky-blue eyes admiring her and before she could even utter a good-morning he'd slipped his hand between her legs. Stroked, rubbed, and brought her to orgasm in less than a minute. As a result, she'd forgotten her name, her surroundings and the reason she'd brought him home in the first place.

Fortunately, the amnesia had been temporary. Her memory had swiftly returned when she'd checked her cell phone messages and saw that both her father and Doug had called.

Brody had made it clear he wanted to see her again, and sure, that would be nice…okay, it would be freaking incredible. But sex wasn't going to solve her problems. Her issues with Doug would still be there, lurking in the wings like a jealous understudy, as would the stress of her father's recent struggles. And if Brody wanted more than sex, if he wanted a relationship (as unlikely as that was) what would she do then? Throw a third complication into her already complicated personal life?

No, ending it before it began was the logical solution. Best to leave it as a one-night stand.

She reached the arena ten minutes later and parked in the area reserved for VIPs, right next to her father's shiny red Mercedes convertible. She knew it was her dad's, because of the license plate reading "TM-OWNR." *Real subtle, Dad.*

Why had she even bothered coming home? When her father had asked if she could take some time off to be with him during this whole divorce mess, she'd seen it as a sign that he valued her support, wanted her around. But in the week she'd been home she'd only seen her dad once, for a quick lunch in his office. The phone had kept ringing, so they'd barely spoken, and it was unlikely they'd get any time to talk tonight. She knew how focused her dad was when he watched hockey.

With a sigh, she got out of the car and braced herself for a night of watching sweaty men skating after a black disk, and listening to her father rave about how "it doesn't get better than this."

Gee, she couldn't wait.

"WATCH OUT FOR Valdek tonight," Sam Becker warned when Brody approached the long wooden bench on one side of the Warriors locker room. He paused in front of his locker.

"Valdek's back?" Brody groaned. "What happened to his three-game suspension?"

Becker adjusted his shin pads then pulled on his navy-blue pants and started lacing up. For thirty-six, he was still in prime condition. When Brody first met the legendary forward he'd been in awe, even more impressed when he'd seen Becker deke out three guys to score a shorthanded goal, proving to everyone in the league why he still belonged there.

And what had impressed him the most was Becker's complete lack of arrogance. Despite winning two championship cups and having a career that rivaled Gretzky's, Sam Becker was as down-to-earth as they came. He was the man everyone went to when they had a problem, whether personal or professional, and over the years, he'd become Brody's closest friend.

"Suspension's over," Becker answered. "And he's out for blood. He hasn't forgotten who got him suspended, kiddo."

Brody ignored the nickname, which Becker refused to ease up on, and snorted. "Right, because it's my fault he sliced my chin open with his skate."

A few more players drifted into the room. The Warriors goalie, Alexi Nicklaus, gave a salute in lieu of greeting. Next to him, Derek Jones, this season's rookie yet already one of the best defensemen in the league, wandered over and said, "Valdek's back."

"So I've heard." Brody peeled his black T-shirt over his head and tossed it on the bench.

Jones suddenly hooted, causing him to glance down at his chest. What he found was a reminder of the most exciting sexual experience of his life. Over his left nipple was the purple hickey Hayden's full lips had branded into his skin, after he'd swooped her off the hallway floor and carried her into the bedroom—where he'd proceeded to make love to her all night long.

This morning he'd woken up to the sight of Hayden's dark hair fanned across the stark white pillow, one bare breast pressing into his chest and a slender leg hooked over his lower body. He'd cuddled after sex plenty of times in the past, but he couldn't remember ever awakening to find himself in the exact post-sex position. Normally he gently rolled his companion over, needing space and distance in order to fall asleep. Last night he hadn't needed it. In fact, he even remembered waking up in the middle of the night and pulling Hayden's warm, naked body closer.

Figure that one out.

"Remind me to keep you away from my daughter," Becker said with a sigh.

Next to him, Jones guffawed. "So who's the lucky lady? Or did you even get her name?"

Brody's back stiffened defensively, but then he wondered why it bothered him that his teammates still viewed him as a playboy. Sure, he *had* been a playboy, once upon a time. When he'd first gone pro, he couldn't help letting it all go to his head. For a kid who'd grown up dirt-poor in Michigan, the sudden onslaught of wealth and attention was like a drug. Exciting. Addictive. Suddenly everyone wanted to be his friend, his confidante, his lover. At twenty-one, he'd welcomed every perk that came with the job—particularly the endless stream of women lining up to warm his bed.

But it'd gotten old once he'd realized that ninety percent of those eager females cared most about his uniform. He didn't mind being in the limelight, but he was no longer interested in going to bed with women who thought of him only as the star forward of the Warriors.

Unfortunately, his teammates couldn't seem to accept that he'd left his playboy days in the dust. It was probably a label thing; the guys on the team liked labels. They all had 'em— Derek Jones was the Prankster, Becker was the Elder, Craig Wyatt was Mr. Serious. And Brody was the Playboy. Apparently admitting otherwise screwed up the team dynamic or something.

Ah, well. Let them believe what they wanted. He might not be a Casanova anymore but he could still kick their butts any day of the week.

"Yes, I got her name," he said, rolling his eyes.

Just not her number.

He kept that irksome detail to himself. He still wasn't sure why it bugged him, Hayden's refusal to give him her phone number. And for the life of him, he also couldn't make sense of that bomb of a speech she'd dropped on him earlier.

I'd rather we didn't see each other again. I had a great time, but I never had any intention of this going beyond one night. I hope you understand.

Every man's dream words. He couldn't remember how many times he'd tried to find a way to let a woman down gently when she asked for something more the morning after. Hayden had pretty much summed up the attitude he'd had about sex his entire life. One night, no expectations, nothing more. In the old days he would've sent her a fruit basket with a thank-you card for her casual dismissal.

But these days he wanted more than that. That's why he'd gone back to Hayden's hotel room, because something about the woman made him think she was the one who could give him the *more* he desired. A sexy professor who hated sports and set his body on fire. Almost made him want to call up that *Sports Illustrated* interviewer and get a retraction printed: *Brody Croft is no longer attracted to leggy blondes.*

"Hope you didn't tire yourself out," Becker said. "We can't afford to screw up tonight, not in the play-offs."

"Hey, d'you guys get a look at the paper this morning?" Jones asked suddenly. "There was another article about the bribery accusations Houston's wife made." He frowned, an expression that didn't suit his chubby, *Leave It to Beaver* face. At twenty-one, the kid hadn't mastered his supertough hockey glare yet. "Like any of us would take money to purposely put a loss on our record. Damn, I want to toilet paper that chick's house for all the trouble she's causing."

Brody laughed. "When are you going to grow out of these pranks? Grown men don't toilet paper people's homes."

"C'mon, you like my pranks," Derek protested. "You were laughing your ass off when I replaced Alexi's pads with those pink Hello Kitty ones."

From across the room, their goalie Alexi Nicklaus gave Jones the finger.

"Simmer down, children," Becker said with a grin. He turned to Brody, his eyes suddenly growing serious. "What do you think about the articles?"

Brody just shrugged. "Until I see the proof Mrs. Houston allegedly has, I refuse to believe anybody on this team threw a game."

Jones nodded his agreement. "Pres is a good dude. He'd never fix games." He paused, then chuckled. "Actually, I'm more intrigued by the other allegation. You know, the one from an unnamed source claiming that Mrs. H is hitting the sheets with a Warriors player?"

Huh? Brody hadn't read the paper yet, and the idea that the

owner's wife was sleeping with one of his teammates was both startling and absurd. And worrisome. Definitely worrisome. He didn't like how this scandal seemed to be snowballing. Bribery, adultery, illegal gambling. Shit.

Jones turned to Brody. "Come on, admit it. It was you."

Uh, right. The thought of hopping into the sack with Sheila Houston was about as appealing as trading in his hockey skates for figure skates and joining the Stars on Ice. He'd only needed a handful of encounters with the woman to figure out she had nothing but air between her pretty little ears.

"Nah. My bet's on Topas." Brody grinned at the dark-haired right wing across the room. Zelig Topas, who'd won Olympic silver playing on the Russian team at the last Games, was also one of the few openly gay players in the league.

"Funny," Topas returned, rolling his eyes.

The chatter died down as Craig Wyatt, the captain of the Warriors, strode into the room, his Nordic features solemn as always. Wyatt stood at a massive height of six-seven, and that was in his street shoes. With his bulky torso and blond buzz cut it was no wonder Wyatt was one of the most feared players in the league and a force to contend with.

Without asking what all the laughter was about, Wyatt dove right into his usual pregame pep talk, which was about as peppy as a eulogy. There was a reason Wyatt was nick-named Mr. Serious. Brody had only seen the guy smile once, and even then it was one of those awkward half smiles you pasted on when someone was telling you a really un-funny joke.

Needless to say, Brody had never clicked with his somber captain. He tended to gravitate toward laid-back guys like Becker and Jones.

Promptly tuning out the captain's voice, he proceeded to rehash this morning's conversation with Hayden, musing over her insistence that they leave things at one night. He understood wanting to end with a bang but…

Nope, wasn't going to happen.

Hayden might've neglected to hand out her number, but she'd left her calling card by inviting him to her hotel suite. After tonight's game Brody planned on strolling right back to the Ritz and continuing what he and Hayden had started last night. Just one night?

Not if he could help it.

"THERE'S NOTHING BETTER than this," Presley Houston boomed as he handed his daughter a bottle of Evian and joined her by the glass window overlooking the rink below.

They had the owner's box to themselves tonight, which came as a great relief. When she was surrounded by her father's colleagues, Hayden always felt as if she were one of those whales or dolphins at Sea World. Frolicking, swimming, doing tricks—all the while trying to figure out a way to break through the glass, escape the stifling tank and return to the wild where she belonged.

"Do you get to any games out in California?" Presley asked, picking an imaginary fleck of lint from the front of his gray Armani jacket.

"No, Dad."

"Why the hell not?"

Uh, because I hate hockey and always have?

"I don't have the time. I was teaching four classes last semester."

Her father reached out and ruffled her hair, something he'd done ever since she was a little girl. She found the gesture comforting. It reminded her of the years they'd been close. Before the Warriors. Before Sheila. Back when it was just the two of them.

Her heart ached as her dad tucked a strand of hair behind her ear and shot her one of his charming smiles. And her father undeniably had charm. Despite the loud booming voice, the restless energy he seemed to radiate, the focused and often shrewd glint in his eyes, he had a way of making everyone around him feel like he was their best friend. It was probably why his players seemed to idolize him, and definitely why *she* had idolized him growing up. She'd never thought her dad was perfect. He'd dragged her around the country for his career. But he'd also been there when it counted, helping with her homework, letting her take art classes during the off-season, giving her that painful birds-and-bees talk kids always got from their parents.

It brought a knot of pain to her gut that her father didn't seem to notice the distance between them. Not that she expected them to be bosom buddies—she was an adult now, and leading her own life. Nevertheless, it would be nice to at least maintain some kind of friendship with her dad. But he lived and breathed the Warriors now, completely oblivious to the fact that he'd pushed his only daughter onto the back burner of his life these past seven years.

She noticed that gray threads of hair were beginning to appear at his temples. She'd seen him six months ago over Christmas, but somehow he seemed older. There were even wrinkles around his mouth that hadn't been there before. The divorce proceedings were evidently taking a toll on him.

"Sweetheart, I know this might not be the best time to bring this up," her father began suddenly, averting his eyes. He focused on the spectacle of the game occurring below, as if he could channel the energy of the players and find the nerve to continue. Finally he did. "One of the reasons I asked you to come home…well, see…Diane wants you to give a deposition."

Her head jerked up. "What? Why?"

"You were one of the witnesses the day Sheila signed the prenuptial agreement." Her dad's voice was gentler than she'd heard in years. "Do you remember?"

Uh, did he actually think she'd forget? The day they'd signed the prenup happened to be the first meeting between Hayden and her only-two-years-older stepmother. The shock that her fifty-seven-year-old father was getting remarried after years of being alone hadn't been as great as learning that he was marrying a woman so many years his junior. Hayden had prided herself on being open-minded, but her mind always seemed to slam shut the second her father was involved. Although Sheila claimed otherwise, Hayden wasn't convinced that her stepmother hadn't married Presley for his money, prenup or not.

Her suspicions had been confirmed when three months into the marriage, Sheila convinced her father to buy a multimillion-dollar mansion (because living in a penthouse was *so* passé), a small yacht (because the sea air would do them good) and a brand-new wardrobe (because the wife of a sports team owner needed to look sharp). Hayden didn't even want to know how much money her dad had spent on Sheila that first year. Even if she worked until she was ninety, she'd probably never earn that much. Sheila, of course, had quit her waitressing job the day after the wedding, and as far as Hayden knew, her stepmother now spent her days shopping away Presley's money.

"Do I really have to get involved in this, Dad?" she asked, sighing.

"It's just one deposition, sweetheart. All you have to do is go on record and state that Sheila was in her right mind when she signed those papers." Presley made a rude sound. "She's claiming coercion was involved."

"Oh, Dad. Why did you marry that woman?"

Her father didn't answer, and she didn't blame him. He'd always been a proud man, and admitting his failures came as naturally to him as the ability to give birth.

"This won't go to court, will it?" Her stomach turned at the thought.

"I doubt it." He ruffled her hair again. "Diane is confident we'll be able to reach a settlement. Sheila can't go on like this forever. Sooner or later she'll give up."

Not likely.

She kept her suspicions to herself, not wanting to upset her father any further. She could tell by the frustration in his eyes that the situation was making him feel powerless. And she knew how much he hated feeling powerless.

Hayden gave his arm a reassuring squeeze. "Of course she will." She gestured to the window. "By the way, the team's looking really great, Dad."

She had no clue about whether the team looked good or not, but her words brought a smile to her father's lips and that was all that mattered.

"They are, aren't they? Wyatt and Becker are really coming together this season. Coach Gray said it was tough going, trying to make them get along."

"They don't like each other?" she said, not bothering to ask who Wyatt and Becker were.

Her dad shrugged, then took a swig from the glass of bourbon in his hand. "You know how it is, sweetheart. Alpha males, I'm-the-best, no-I'm-the-best. The league is nothing more than an association of egos."

"Dad..." She searched for the right words. "That stuff in the paper yesterday, about the illegal betting...it's not true, is it?"

"Of course not." He scowled. "It's lies, Hayden. All a bunch of lies."

"You sure I shouldn't be worried?"

He pulled her close, squeezing her shoulder. "There is absolutely nothing for you to worry about. I promise."

"Good."

A deafening buzz followed by a cheesy dance beat interrupted their conversation. In a second Presley was on his feet, clapping and giving a thumbs-up to the camera that seemed to float past the window.

"Did we win?" she asked, feeling stupid for asking and even stupider for not knowing.

Her father chuckled. "Not yet. There's five minutes left to the third." He returned to his seat. "When the game's done how about I take you for a quick tour of the arena? We've done a lot of renovations since you were last here. Sound good?"

"Sounds great," she lied.

BRODY STEPPED out of the shower and drifted back to the main locker area. He pressed his hand to his side and winced at the jolt of pain that followed. A glance down confirmed what he already knew—that massive check from Valdek at the beginning of the second period had resulted in a large bruise that was slowly turning purple. Asshole.

"You took a shitty penalty," Wyatt was grumbling to Jones when Brody reached the bench.

The captain's normally calm voice contained a hint of antagonism and his dark eyes flashed with disapproval, also uncharacteristic. Brody wondered what was up Wyatt's ass, but he preferred to stay out of quarrels between his teammates. Hockey players were wired to begin with, so minor disagreements often ended badly.

Derek rolled his eyes. "What are you complaining about? We won the freaking game."

"It could've been a shutout," Wyatt snapped. "You gave up a goal to Franks with that penalty. We might be up by two games, but we need to win two more to make it to the second round. There's no room for mistakes." Still glowering, Mr. Serious strode out of the locker room, slamming the door behind him.

Jones tossed a what-the-hell's-up-with-him? look in Brody's direction, but he just shrugged, still determined to stay out of it.

Dressing quickly, he shoved his sweaty uniform into the locker, suddenly eager to get out of there.

On his way to the door he checked his watch, which read nine forty-five. Too late to pay a visit to Hayden's penthouse suite? Probably. Maybe inappropriate, too, but, hell, he'd never been one for propriety. Hayden had been on his mind all day and he was determined to see her again.

"Later, boys," he called over his shoulder.

The door closed behind him and he stepped into the brightly lit hallway, promptly colliding with a warm wall of curves.

"I'm sor—" The apology died in his throat as he laid eyes on the woman he'd bodychecked.

Not just any woman, either, but the one he'd been thinking about—and getting hard over—all day.

A startled squeak flew out of her mouth. "You."

His surprise quickly transformed into a rush of satisfaction and pleasure. "Me," he confirmed.

Looking her up and down, Brody was taken aback by the prim white blouse she wore and the knee-length paisley skirt that swirled over her legs. A huge change from the bright yellow top and faded jeans she'd worn last night. In this getup she looked more like the conservative professor and less like the passionate vixen who'd cried out his name so many times last night. The shift was disconcerting.

"What are…you're…" Hayden's eyes darted to the sign on the door beside them. "You play for the Warriors?"

"Sure do." He lifted one brow. "And I thought you said you weren't a hockey fan."

"I'm not. I…" Her voice trailed off.

What was she doing in this section of the arena? he suddenly wondered. Only folks associated with the franchise were allowed back here.

"Sorry to keep you waiting, sweetheart," boomed a male voice. "Shall we continue the tour—" Presley Houston broke out in a wide smile when he noticed Brody. "You played well out there tonight, Croft."

"Thanks, Pres." He looked from Hayden to Presley, wondering if he was missing something. Then a hot spurt of jealousy erupted in his gut as he realized that Presley had called Hayden *sweetheart.* Oh, man. Had he screwed around with Houston's mistress?

A dose of anger joined the jealousy swirling through him. He eyed the woman he'd spent the night with, wanting to strangle her for hopping into bed with him when she was obviously very much *taken,* but Presley's next words quickly killed the urge and brought with them another shock.

"I see you've met my daughter, Hayden."

4

WHAT WAS HE *doing* here? And why hadn't he told her he played for the Warriors?

Hayden blinked a few times. Maybe she was imagining his sleek, long body and devastatingly handsome face and the hair that curled under his ears as if he'd just stepped out of a steamy shower—

He's not a hallucination. Deal with it.

All right, so her one-night stand was undeniably here, flesh and blood, and sexier than ever.

He also happened to be one of her dad's players. Was there a section in the league rule book about a player sleeping with the team owner's daughter? She didn't think so, but with all the rumors currently circulating about her father and the franchise, Hayden didn't feel inclined to cause any more trouble for her dad.

Apparently Brody felt the same way.

"It's nice to meet you, Hayden." His voice revealed nothing, especially not the fact that they were already very much…acquainted, for lack of a better word.

She shook his hand, almost shivering at the feel of his warm, calloused fingers. "Charmed," she said lightly.

Charmed? Had she actually just said that?

Brody's eyes twinkled, confirming that the idiotic reply had indeed come out of her mouth.

"Hayden is visiting us from San Francisco," Presley explained. "She teaches art at Berkeley."

"Art history, Dad," she corrected.

Presley waved a dismissive hand. "Same difference."

"So what position do you play?" Hayden asked, her voice casual, neutral, as if she were addressing a complete stranger.

"Brody's a left winger," Presley answered for him. "And a rising star."

"Oh. Sounds exciting," she said mildly.

Presley cut in once more. "It is. Right, Brody?"

Before Brody could answer, someone else snagged her dad's attention. "There's Stan. Excuse me for a moment." He quickly marched away.

Hayden's mouth curved mischievously. "Don't mind him. He often takes over conversations only to leave you standing in his dust." Her smile faded. "But you probably already knew that, seeing as you play for his team."

"Does that bother you?" Brody said carefully.

"Of course not," she lied. "Why would it?"

"You tell me."

She stared at him for a moment, then sighed. "Look, I'd appreciate it if you didn't tell my father about what…happened between us last night."

"Ah, so you remember." Amusement danced in his eyes. "I was starting to think you'd put it out of your mind completely."

Sure. Like that was even possible. She'd thought about nothing but this man and his talented tongue all day.

"I haven't forgotten." Her voice lowered. "But that doesn't mean I want to do it again."

"I think you do."

The arrogance in his tone both annoyed her and thrilled her. Jeez, how *hadn't* she figured out he was a hockey player last night? The man practically had *pro athlete* branded into his forehead. He was cocky, confident, larger than life. Something told her he was the kind of man who knew exactly what he wanted and did everything in his power to get it.

And what he wanted at the moment, disconcerting as it was, seemed to be *her*.

"Brody—"

"Don't bother denying it, I rocked your world last night and you can't wait for me to do it again."

She snorted. "There's nothing like a man with a healthy ego."

"I like it when you snort. It's cute."

"Don't call me cute."

"Why not?"

"Because I hate it. Babies and bunny rabbits are cute. I'm a grown woman. And stop looking at me like that."

"Like what?" he said, blinking innocently.

"Like you're imagining me naked."

"I can't help it. I *am* imagining you naked."

His eyes darkened to a sensual glitter, and liquid heat promptly pooled between her thighs. She tried not to squeeze her legs together. She didn't want him seeing the effect he had on her.

"Have a drink with me tonight," he said suddenly.

The word *no* slipped out more quickly than she'd intended.

Brody's features creased with what looked like frustration. He stepped closer, causing her to dart a glance in her father's direction. Presley was standing at the end of the hall, engaged in deep conversation with Stan Gray, the Warriors' head coach. While her dad seemed oblivious to the sparks shooting between her and Brody, Hayden still felt uncomfortable having this discussion in view of her father.

It didn't help that Brody looked so darn edible in gray wool pants that hugged his muscular legs and a ribbed black sweater that stretched across his chest. And his wet hair… She forced herself to stop staring at those damp strands, knowing that if she allowed herself to imagine him in the shower, naked, she might just come on the spot.

"One drink," he insisted, with a charming grin. "You know, for old time's sake."

She couldn't help but laugh. "We've known each other for all of twenty-four hours."

"Yes, but it was a very wild twenty-four hours, wouldn't you say?" He moved closer and lowered his head, his lips inches from her ear, his warm breath fanning across her neck. "How many times did you come again, Hayden? Three? Four?"

"Five," she squeezed out, and then quickly looked around to make sure nobody had heard her.

Her entire body started to throb from the memory. Nipples hardened. Sex grew moist. That she could experience such arousal in a hallway full of people—one of them her father— made her blush with embarrassment.

"Five." He nodded briskly. "I haven't lost my touch."

She resisted the urge to groan. He was too damn sexual, too sure of himself, which gave him a definite advantage, because at the moment she wasn't sure of anything.

Except the fact that she wanted to tear off her clothes and hop right back into bed with Brody Croft.

But, nope, she wouldn't do it. Sleeping with Brody again had Bad Idea written all over it. It had all been much simpler last night, when he'd just been an exciting, sensual stranger. But now…now he was real. Even worse, he was a hockey player. She'd grown up around enough hockey players to know how they lived—the constant traveling, the media, the eager females lining up to jump into bed with them.

And along with being involved in a sport she hated, Brody was so…arrogant, flirtatious, bold. Yesterday it had added to the allure of sex with a stranger. Today it was a reminder of why she'd decided bad boys no longer played a part in her life.

Been there, done that. Her last boyfriend had been as arrogant, flirty and bold as Brody Croft, and that relationship had ended a fiery death when Adam dumped her on her birthday because the whole "fidelity thing" cramped his style. His words, not hers.

She wasn't quite sure why she had such terrible judgment when it came to men. It shouldn't be so hard finding someone to build a life with, should it? A home, a solid marriage, great sex, excitement *and* stability, a man who'd make their relationship a priority—was that too much to ask for?

"Why are you so determined to see me again?" she found herself blurting, then lowered her voice when her father glanced in their direction. "I told you this morning I wanted to leave things at one night."

"What about what I want?"

She bit back an annoyed curse, deciding to go for the honest approach. "My life is complicated right now," she admitted. "I came home to support my father, not get involved with someone."

"You were pretty involved with me last night," he said, winking. He uncrossed his arms and let them drop to his sides. "And you can't deny you liked it, Hayden."

"Of course I liked it," she hissed.

"Then what's the problem?"

"The problem is, I wanted one night. Seeing you again wasn't part of the plan."

"Plan, or fantasy?" he drawled, a knowing glimmer in his eyes. "That's it, isn't it? You fantasized about indulging in one night of wicked sex with a stranger and now that you have it it's time to move on. I'm not judging you, just pointing out that the fantasy doesn't have to end yet."

The word *fantasy* sounded intoxicating the way he said it. Before she could stop herself, she wondered what other fantasies they could play out together. Role play? Bondage? Her cheeks grew warm at the latter notion. It turned her on, the idea of tying Brody up…straddling him while he lay immobile on the bed…

No. No, she was *so* not going there. She seriously needed to quit letting this guy jump-start her sex drive.

"The way I see it, you've got two options," he said. "The easy way or the hard way."

"I can't wait to hear all about it."

"Sarcasm doesn't become you." His cheek dimpled despite his words. "Now, the easy way involves the two of us heading over to the Lakeshore Lounge for a drink."

"No."

He held up his hand. "You haven't heard the rest." A devilish look flickered across his face. "If you choose to pass on the easy option, that's when things get a little…*hard.*"

Heat spilled over her cheeks. Her eyes dropped to his groin, almost expecting to see the long ridge of arousal pressing against the denim of his jeans. Fine, no almost about it. He had an erection, all right, and the second she noticed it her nipples grew even harder.

"See, if you deny me this one harmless drink," he continued, "I'll be hurt. Maybe even a tad offended. Also, your father seems to be nearing the end of his conversation—yup, he's shaking Stan's hand. Which means he'll head back over here just in time to hear you say no, and then he'll ask you what you're saying no to, and I'm sure neither one of us wants to open *that* can of worms."

She turned her head and, sure enough, her father was walking toward them. Great. Although she knew her dad could handle the knowledge that his twenty-six-year-old daughter wasn't a virgin, she didn't want him privy to her sex life. Especially a sex life that involved one of his players.

Her dad might be totally gaga over his team, but he'd often warned her about the turbulent nature of hockey players. The latest warning had come during her last visit to Chicago, when she'd been hit on by an opposing player after a Warriors game. She'd declined the dinner invitation, but it hadn't stopped Presley from launching into a speech about how he didn't want his daughter dating brutes.

If he knew she'd gotten involved with Brody, it would just add to his stress.

"So how about that drink, Hayden?"

Her pulse quickened when she realized if she agreed to Brody's request, chances were they wouldn't get around to the drink anyway. The second he had her alone he'd be slipping his hands underneath her shirt, palming her breasts, sucking on her neck the way he'd done last night, as he'd slid inside her and—

"One drink," she blurted, then chastised herself for yet again letting her hormones override her common sense. What was *wrong* with her?

With a soft chuckle, Brody rested his hands on his trim hips, the poster boy for cool. "I knew you'd see it my way." He grinned.

THE LAKESHORE LOUNGE WAS one of those rare bars in the city that offered an intimate atmosphere rather than an intrusive one. Plush, comfortable chairs looked more suited to an IKEA showroom; tables were situated far enough apart that patrons could enjoy their drinks in privacy, and a pale yellow glow took the place of bright lighting, providing an almost sensual ambience. It was also one of the only establishments that still adhered to a strict dress code—blazers required.

It was a damn good thing he was Brody Croft. Even better

that Ward Dalton, the owner of the lounge, claimed to be his number-one fan and turned a blind eye to Brody's casual attire.

Dalton led them across the black marble floor to a secluded table in the corner of the room, practically hidden from view by two enormous stone pots containing leafy indoor palms. A waiter clad in black pants and a white button-down appeared soon after, taking their drink orders before unobtrusively moving away.

Brody didn't miss the baffled look on Hayden's gorgeous face. "Something wrong?" he asked.

"No. I'm just…surprised," she said. "When you said we were going for a drink, I thought…" Her cheeks turned an appealing shade of pink. "Forget it."

"You thought I'd drive you right back to your hotel suite and pick up where we left off?"

"Pretty much."

"Sorry to disappoint you."

She bristled at the teasing lilt of his voice. "I'm not disappointed. In fact, I'm glad. Like I said before, I'm not interested in getting involved."

He didn't like the finality of her tone. For the life of him, he couldn't figure out why Hayden didn't want a repeat performance of last night. They'd been so good together.

He also couldn't decide whether or not she'd known who he was all along. Her father was Presley Houston, for chrissake. She didn't need to *like* hockey to know who the players were, especially the players on her own father's team. And yet the shock on her face when she'd bumped into him outside the locker room hadn't seemed contrived. He'd seen authentic surprise on her beautiful face. Not to mention a flicker of dismay.

No, she couldn't have known. It wouldn't bother her this much if she had.

He appreciated that she liked the man and not the hockey

player, but that only raised another question—what held her back from getting involved with him? Was it the fact that he played pro hockey, or was it something else? *Someone* else, perhaps?

His jaw tightened at the thought. "What exactly is stopping you from pursuing this?" he asked in a low voice. "It's more than Presley's current problems, isn't it?"

The way she stared down at the silk cocktail napkin on the table as if it were the most fascinating item on the planet deepened Brody's suspicions.

He narrowed his eyes, unable to keep the accusation out of his tone. "Is there a husband waiting for you in California?"

Her gaze flew up to meet his. "Of course not."

Some of the suspicion thawed, but not entirely. "A fiancé?"

She shook her head.

"A boyfriend?"

The blush on her cheeks deepened. "No. I mean, yes. Well, kind of. I *was* seeing someone in San Francisco but we're currently on a break."

"The kind of break where you can sleep with other people?"

Whoa, he had no idea why he'd become antagonistic, or why his shoulders were suddenly stiffer than Robocop's.

What was up with this sudden possessiveness? They'd only had one night together, after all. Staking claims at this point was ridiculous.

"As I keep telling you, my life is complicated," she said pointedly. "I'm in the process of making some serious decisions, figuring out what my future looks like."

He opened his mouth to reply only to be interrupted by the waiter, who returned with their drinks. The waiter set down Brody's gin and tonic and Hayden's glass of white wine, then left the table without delay, as if sensing something important was brewing between them.

"And this boyfriend," Brody said thoughtfully. "Do you see him in your future?"

"I don't know."

Her tentative answer and confused frown were all he needed. He wasn't an ass; if Hayden had expressed deep love for the other man in her life, Brody would've backed off. He had no interest in fighting for a woman who belonged to someone else. But the fact that she hadn't answered a definite yes to his question told Brody this was fair game.

And nothing got him going more than a healthy bout of competition.

He lifted his gin and tonic to his lips and took a sip, eyeing her from the rim of his glass. Despite her prim shirt that buttoned up to the neck, she looked unbelievably hot. He could see the outline of her bra, and the memory of what lay beneath it sent a jolt of electricity to his groin.

"We're not doing it again," she said between gritted teeth, obviously sensing the train of thought his mind had taken.

He laughed. "Sounds like you're trying to convince yourself of that."

Frustration creased her dainty features. "We had sex, Brody. That's all." She took a drink of wine. "It was amazing, sure, but it was only sex. It's not like the damn earth moved."

"Are you sure about that?"

He pushed his chair closer, so that they were no longer across from each other, but side by side. He saw her hands shake at his nearness, her cheeks flush again, her lips part. It didn't take a rocket scientist to see she was aroused, and, damn, but he liked knowing his mere proximity could get this woman going.

"It was more than sex, Hayden." He dipped his head and brushed his lips over her ear. She shivered. "It was a sexual hurricane. Intense. Consuming." He flicked his tongue against her earlobe. "I've never been that hard in my life. And you've never been wetter."

"Brody…" She swallowed.

He traced the shell of her ear with his tongue, then moved his head back and lowered his hand to her thigh. He felt her leg shaking under his touch. "I'm right, aren't I?"

"Fine," she blurted out. "You're right! Happy?"

"Not quite." With a faint smile, he slid his hand under the soft material of her skirt and cupped her mound. Running his knuckles against the damp spot on her panties, he gave a brisk nod and murmured, "Now I'm happy."

Hayden's focus darted around like a Ping-Pong ball, as if she expected their waiter to pop up in front of them any second. But the table was well secluded, and nobody could approach it without entering Brody's line of sight. He took advantage of the privacy, cupping Hayden's ass and gently shifting her so that her body was more accessible. He dragged his hand between her legs again, pushing aside the crotch of her panties and stroking her damp flesh.

The soft sounds of people chatting at neighboring tables excited the hell out of him. He was no stranger to sex in public, but he couldn't say he'd ever pleasured a woman in an upscale bar where any minute he could get caught.

A sharp breath hissed out of her mouth as he rubbed her clit in a circular motion. "What are you doing?" she whispered.

"I think you know exactly what I'm doing."

He continued to boldly rub her clit, then danced his finger-tips down her slick folds and prodded her opening with the tip of his index finger. The wetness already pooling there made his cock twitch. He wanted nothing more than to shuck his jeans and thrust into that wet paradise. Right here. Right now. But he wasn't *that* bold.

"Brody…you've got…to stop," she murmured, but her body said otherwise.

Her thighs clenched together, her inner muscles squeezed his finger and a soft moan slipped out of her throat.

"You'll come if I keep doing this, won't you, Hayden?"

He looked from her flushed face to the neighboring table, several feet away and barely visible through the palm fronds separating the two tables. He hoped to hell the couple seated at that table hadn't heard Hayden's moan. He didn't want this to end just yet.

"Brody, anyone can walk by."

"Then you'd better be quick."

He pushed his finger into her core, smiling when she bit her lip. The look on her face drove him wild. Flushed, tortured, excited. He was feeling pretty excited himself, but he managed to get a handle on his own rising desire. He'd pressured her to spend the evening with him because he had something to prove, and what he wanted to prove wasn't that he was dying for a second go, but that *she* was dying for it.

Applying pressure to her clit with his thumb, he worked another finger inside her, pushing in and out of her in a deliberate lazy rhythm. His mouth ached with the need to suck on one of her small pink nipples, but he tightened his lips before he gave in to the urge and tore her shirt open. Instead, he focused on the heat between her thighs, the nub that swelled each time he brushed his thumb over it and the inner walls that clamped over his fingers with each gentle thrust.

Keeping one eye on Hayden's blissful face and the other on his surroundings, he continued to slide his fingers in and out, until finally she let out a barely audible groan and squeezed her legs together. He felt her pulsing against his fingers and resisted a groan of his own as a soundless orgasm consumed her eyes as well as her body.

She came silently, trembling, biting her lip. And then she released a sigh. Her hands, which at some point she'd curled into fists, shook on the tabletop, making her wineglass topple and spill over the side of the table.

He quickly withdrew his hand as Hayden jumped at the startling sound of the glass rolling and shattering on the marble floor. Her sudden movement caused her knee to hit one of the table legs, making the table shake and the ice cubes in his drink collide into the side of the glass with a jingling sound.

From the corner of his eye Brody saw the waiter hurrying over, and yet he couldn't fight a tiny chuckle. Turning to meet Hayden's dazed eyes, he laughed again, swiftly fixed her skirt and said, "Still want to tell me the earth didn't move?"

5

ABOUT TWELVE HOURS after experiencing her very first public orgasm, Hayden strode into Lingerie Dreams, the classy downtown boutique owned by her best friend.

She was in desperate need of Darcy right now. Darcy and her one-night-stand mentality would definitely help her get her thoughts back on the right track and *off* the track that sent her hurtling straight into Brody Croft's bed.

Funny thing was, he hadn't pushed her after their interlude at the lounge last night. He'd paid for their drinks, walked her out to her rental car and left her with a parting speech she couldn't stop thinking about.

The next move's yours, Hayden. You want me, come and get me.

And then he'd left. He'd hopped into his shiny SUV, driven off and left her sitting in her car, more turned-on than she'd ever been in her entire life. Though she'd been ready to go home with him, he'd made it clear it wouldn't happen that night, not when he'd had to twist her arm to get her there.

Oh, no, he wanted *her* to initiate their next encounter. Something she was seriously tempted to do. Which was why she needed Darcy to talk her out of it.

The bell over the door chimed as she walked into the boutique. She sidestepped a mannequin wearing a black lace teddy and a table piled high with thongs, and approached the cash counter.

"Something terrible has happened," Darcy groaned the second she saw her.

"Tell me about it," Hayden mumbled.

But the look of dismay on Darcy's face made Hayden push the memory of last night aside for the moment. She caught a whiff of sweet floral scent, looked around and finally spotted a bouquet of red and yellow roses peeking out of the metal wastebasket next to the counter.

"Courtesy of Jason," Darcy sighed, following her gaze.

"Who's Jason?"

"Didn't I mention him?" She shrugged. "I hooked up with him last week after yoga class. He's a personal trainer."

Like she could actually keep track of all the men Darcy hooked up with. Hayden didn't know how her friend did it, wandering aimlessly from guy to guy.

"And he sent you flowers? That's sweet."

Darcy looked at her as if she'd grown horns. "Are you insane?" she said. "Don't you remember how I feel about flowers?"

Without waiting for an answer, Darcy leapt to her feet and checked to make sure the store was void of customers. Then she marched over to the front door, locked it and flipped the Open sign over so that it read Closed.

With her kitten heels clicking against the tiled floor, Darcy gestured for Hayden to follow her, drifting over to the fitting-room area. Along with four dressing rooms, the large space offered two plush red velvet chairs.

Hayden sank into one of the chairs and reached for the bowl of heart-shaped mints Darcy left out for her customers. Popping a mint into her mouth, she studied her friend, who still looked upset.

"Wow, this flower thing is really bugging you."

Darcy flopped down and crossed her arms over her chest,

her face turning as red as the hair on her head. "Of course it bugs me. It's not normal."

"No, *you're* not normal. Men give women flowers all the time. It's not poor Jason's fault he picked you as the recipient."

"We went out for smoothies after yoga and fooled around in his car when he dropped me off at home." Darcy made a frustrated sound. "How in bloody hell does that warrant flowers?"

"What did the card say?" Hayden asked curiously.

"'I hope to see you again soon.'"

She was about to comment on Jason's thoughtfulness again but stopped herself. She knew how Darcy felt about relationships. The first sign of commitment had her fleeing for the exit and looking for the next one-night stand. But it really was too bad. This Jason fellow sounded as nice as Doug.

Shoot, she'd promised herself she wouldn't think about Doug today.

She still hadn't returned his phone call, and when she'd woken up this morning there had been another message from him on her cell. How could she call him back, though? She'd only been gone a week and already she'd jumped into bed with another man. She wondered how nice Doug would be when she told him about *that*.

"I'm going to have to find a new gym," Darcy grumbled, her blue eyes darkening with irritation. She started fidgeting. Crossed her legs, then uncrossed them, clasped her hands together, then drummed them against the arms of the chair.

Hayden could tell her friend was about to explode. Any minute now…no, any second now…

"What is the *matter* with the penis species?" Darcy burst out. "They claim that *we're* the needy ones, calling us clingy and high-maintenance, accusing us of being obsessed with love and marriage. When really, really, it's what *they* want. They're the mushy ones, sending flowers as if a smoothie and a backseat blow job qualify as a monumental event that needs to be celebrated…" Darcy's voice trailed and she heaved a sigh.

"I'm obviously going to have to set him straight," Darcy declared, reaching for a mint and shoving it into her mouth. She still looked aggravated, but her anger seemed to have dissolved.

"At least thank him for the flowers," Hayden said gently.

"I already called and did that. But I think I need to make another call and make sure Jason knows what happened between us won't go any further. Like the way you set your hunk straight."

"Right. About that…you're not going to believe this." She quickly filled her friend in on her visit to the arena and how she'd run into Brody outside the locker room.

"He's a hockey player? I bet you were just thrilled to find that out." Darcy grinned. "So, you told him to get lost, right?"

"Um…"

Darcy's jaw dropped. "Hayden Lorraine Houston! You slept with him again, didn't you?"

"Not exactly. I did go out for a drink with him, though."

"And?"

Hayden told her about the under-the-table orgasm. When her friend shook her head, she added, "I couldn't help it! He just started…you know…and it was really good…" Her voice drifted.

"You have no self-control." Darcy shot her a weary look and asked, "Are you going to call him?"

"I don't know. God knows I want to. But calling him defeats the purpose of a one-night stand." She groaned. "I just wanted some stress-busting sex. And now I'm even more stressed-out."

"So tell him to take a hike. You've got enough on your plate without an arrogant hockey player demanding overtime sex."

Hayden laughed. "He is pretty determined." She remembered the passion flaring in his eyes when he'd brought her to climax yesterday. "He's driving me crazy, Darce."

"Good crazy or bad crazy?"

"Both." A shaky breath exited her throat. "When I'm with him all I can think about is ripping off his clothes, and when I'm not with him all I can think about is ripping off his clothes."

"I don't see the bad part here."

She bit her bottom lip. "He's a hockey player. You know how I feel about that." She blew out a frustrated breath. "I don't want to be with anyone involved in sports. God, I hated it when Dad used to coach. No real place to call home, no friends. Hell, my friendship with you is the only one that lasted, and half of it took place via e-mail."

Reaching for another mint, she popped it into her mouth and bit it in half, taking out her frustration on the candy. "I don't want to date a guy who spends half the year flying to other states so he can skate around an ice rink. And besides, I'm dealing with too much other stuff at the moment. The franchise is taking some heat, Dad's dumping all his Sheila problems on me, and Doug has already called twice wanting to talk about *us.* I can't launch myself into another relationship right now." She set her jaw, practically daring Darcy to challenge her.

Which, of course, she did. "You know what I think?" Darcy said. "You're making too big a deal out of this."

"Oh, really?"

Darcy leaned back in her chair and pushed a strand of bright red hair behind her ear. "You're only in town for a couple of months, Hayden. What's the problem with having some fun in the sack while you're here?"

"What happened to your one-night-stand speech?"

"Apparently it isn't working out for you." Darcy shrugged. "But you seem to believe it's black and white, one-night stand or relationship. You're forgetting about the gray area between the two extremes."

"Gray area?"

"It's called a fling."

"A fling." She said the word slowly, trying it on for size. She'd never been a casual-fling girl, but then again, she hadn't thought she was a one-night girl, either. Maybe a fling with Brody wouldn't be so disastrous. It wasn't like he wanted to marry her or anything; he just wanted to burn up the sheets for a while longer, continue the fantasy…

But if she agreed to let their one night lead into a fling, who's to say the fling wouldn't then lead to something more?

"I don't know," she said. "Brody is a distraction I can't deal with at the moment." She paused, her mouth twisting ruefully. "But my body seems to have a mind of its own whenever he's around."

"So take control of your body," Darcy suggested.

"And how do I do that?"

"I don't know, next time you get the urge to jump Brody Croft's bones, try an alternative. Watch some porn or something."

A laugh tickled Hayden's throat. "That's your answer? Watch porn?"

Darcy grinned. "Sure. At least you won't be thinking about Mr. Hockey when you're busy getting turned-on by other men."

"Right, because the men in porn are so wildly attractive," Hayden said with a snort. "What's the name of that guy who used to be really popular, the chubby one with the facial hair? Ron Jeremy?"

"It's not the seventies, hon. Male porn stars have come a long way. Trust me, just take a long bubble bath, put in a DVD and go nuts. You won't think about Brody even once."

"This is possibly the most ridiculous conversation we've

ever had." Hayden rolled her eyes. "If I watch anything tonight, it'll be the van Gogh special on the Biography Channel."

Darcy released an exaggerated sigh. "A man who cut off his own ear is not sexy, Hayden."

"Neither is porn." She glanced at her watch, eyes widening. "Shoot. I've gotta go. I'm supposed to give a deposition today about Sheila's state of mind when she signed the prenup."

"Sounds like a blast. Unfortunately I left my party shoes at home so I can't come with you."

They got up and wandered over to the door. Darcy unlocked it and held it open, her attention straying back to the flowers poking out of the wastebasket. "At least your guy only wants sex," Darcy said, looking envious.

"Brody is not my guy," Hayden responded, hoping if she said the words out loud she might convince her traitorous body of it. "Are we still on for dinner tonight? I'm down as long as I get home in time to watch that biography."

"And I'm down as long as it's Mexican. I'm feeling spicy." Darcy waved as Hayden left. "Enjoy the deposition," she called out after her.

"Enjoy the flowers," Hayden called back.

She turned just in time to see her best friend flipping her the bird.

"THANK YOU, Hayden," announced Diane Krueger, Presley's divorce attorney. "We're finished here."

Hayden smoothed out the front of her knee-length black skirt and pushed back the plush chair, getting to her feet. Next to her, her father stood as well. On the other side of the large oval conference table of the Krueger and Bates deposition room, Sheila Houston and her lawyer were huddled together, whispering to each other.

Hayden couldn't help but stare at her stepmother, still as

startled by Sheila's appearance as she'd been when the woman had first strode into the law office. The last time Hayden had come to town, Sheila had looked as if she'd stepped from the pages of a fashion magazine. Long blond hair brushed to a shine, creamy features flawless and perfectly made up, expensive clothes hugging her tall, slender body.

This time Sheila looked…haggard. Much older than her twenty-eight years and far more miserable than Hayden had expected her to be. Her hair hung limply over her shoulders, her normally dazzling blue eyes were distressed, and she'd lost at least fifteen pounds, which made her willowy shape look far too fragile.

Though she hated feeling even an ounce of sympathy for the woman who was making her father's life hell, Hayden had to wonder if Sheila was taking this divorce process a lot harder than Presley had let on. Either that, or she was devastated by the thought of losing that yacht she'd forced Presley to buy.

"Thanks for doing this, sweetheart," her father said quietly as they exited the conference room. "It means so much that you're going to bat for your old man."

For the third time in the past hour, Hayden noticed her dad's slightly glazed, bloodshot eyes and wondered if he'd had something to drink before coming here. His breath smelled like toothpaste and cigars, but she got a wary feeling when she looked at him.

No, she was being silly. He was probably just tired.

"I'm happy to help," she answered with a reassuring smile.

He touched her arm. "Do you need a ride back to the suite?"

"No, I've got my rental."

"All right." He nodded. "And don't forget about the party on Sunday night. Gallagher Club, eight o'clock."

Shoot, she'd already forgotten. There was a huge shindig at the prestigious gentlemen's club of which her dad was a member. And apparently her appearance was necessary, though she had no clue why.

Her father must have noticed her reluctance because he frowned slightly. "I'd like you to be there, Hayden. A lot of my friends want to see you. When you were here over the holidays you declined all of their invitations."

Because I wanted to see you, she almost blurted. But she held her tongue. She knew her father liked showing her off to his wealthy friends and boasting about her academic credentials—something he didn't seem to care about when they were alone.

She swallowed back the slight sting of bitterness. Considering they'd just spent an hour with the woman determined to bleed him dry, Hayden figured she ought to cut her dad some slack.

"I'll be there," she promised.

"Good."

They said their goodbyes, and she watched her father hurry out of the elegant lobby onto the street as if he were being chased by a serial killer. Not a stretch, seeing as the law firm was called Krueger and Bates. Hayden wondered if she was the only one who'd made the connection.

"Hayden, wait."

She stopped at the massive glass entrance doors, suppressing an inward groan at the sound of her stepmother's throaty voice.

Hayden turned slowly.

"I just…" Sheila looked surprisingly nervous as she plowed ahead. "I wanted to tell you there are no hard feelings. I know you're trying to protect your father."

Hayden's eyebrows said hello to her hairline. No hard feelings? Sheila was in the process of sucking the money out of Presley's bank accounts like a greedy leech and she wanted to make sure there were no hard feelings?

Hayden could only stare.

Sheila hurried on. "I know you've never liked me, and I don't blame you. It's always hard to watch a parent remarry, and I'm sure it doesn't help that I'm only two years older than you." She offered a timid smile.

"We really shouldn't be talking," Hayden said finally, her voice cool. "It's probably a conflict of interest."

"I know." Sheila ran one hand through her hair, her features sad. "But I just wanted you to know that I still care about your father. I care about him a lot."

To Hayden's absolute shock, a couple of tears trickled out of the corners of Sheila's eyes. Even more shocking, the tears didn't look like the crocodile variety.

"If you care, then why are you trying to take everything he owns?" she couldn't help but ask.

A flash of petulant anger crossed Sheila's face. Ah, *here* was the Sheila she knew. Hayden had seen that look plenty of times before, usually when Sheila was trying to convince Presley to buy something outrageous and not getting her way.

"I'm entitled to something," Sheila said defensively, "after everything that man put me through."

Right, because Sheila's life was *so* unpleasant. Living in a mansion, wearing haute couture, not paying a dime for anything…

"I know you think I'm the bad guy here, but you need to know that everything I've done is a result of… No, I'm not going to blame Pres." The tears returned, and Sheila wiped her wet eyes with a shaky hand. "I saw that he was spiraling and I didn't try to help him. I was the one who sent him into another woman's arms."

"Pardon me?" A knot of anger and disbelief twined Hayden's insides together like a pretzel. Sheila was actually insinuating that her father had been the one to stray? Her dislike for the woman quickly doubled. That she could even accuse a man as honorable as Presley Houston of adultery was preposterous.

Sheila eyed her knowingly. "I guess he left out that part."

"I have to get going," Hayden said stiffly, her jaw so tense that her teeth were beginning to ache.

"I don't care what you think of me," Sheila said. "I only want you to take care of your father, Hayden. I think he's started drinking again and I just want to make sure that someone is looking out for him."

Without issuing a goodbye, Sheila pulled an Elvis and left the building.

Hayden watched as her stepmother disappeared down the busy sidewalk, swallowed up by Chicago's afternoon lunch crowd.

She couldn't will herself to move. Lies. It had to be lies. Her father would never break his marriage vows by hopping into bed with another woman. Sheila was in the wrong here. She had to be.

I think he's started drinking again.

The comment replayed in Hayden's brain, making her toy nervously with the hem of her thin blue sweater. She'd thought her father's eyes had looked bleary. Fine, maybe he *did* have a drink or two before coming here, but Sheila's remark implied that Presley's drinking went beyond today. That at some point in time he'd suffered from an alcohol problem.

Was it true? And if so, how hadn't she known about it? She might not visit often, what with her hectic schedule at the university, but she spoke to her father at least once a week and he always sounded normal. *Sober.* Wouldn't she have suspected something if he had a drinking problem?

Lies.

She clung to that one word as she pushed the strap of her

purse higher on her shoulder and stepped through the doors. Sucking in a gust of fresh air, she headed for her rental, force-fully pushing every sentence Sheila had spoken out of her mind.

BRODY LEFT the locker room after a particularly grueling practice, wondering if he'd made a big fat mistake by pretty much telling Hayden the puck was in her end, the next move hers.

It had seemed like the right play at the time, but today, after two hours of tedious drills topped off by a lecture from the coach, he was rethinking the action he'd taken. Or more spe-cifically, regretting the action he wouldn't be getting. His body was sore, his nerves shot, and he knew a few hours in Hayden's bed were all the medicine he needed.

He also knew she wouldn't call.

You got cocky, man.

Was that it? Had he been so confident in his ability to turn Hayden on that he just assumed she'd want him to do it again?

Damn it, why hadn't he taken her home with him? He'd seen the lust in her gorgeous eyes, known that all he had to do was say the word and she'd be in his arms again, but he'd held back. No, pride had held him back. He hadn't wanted to go to bed with her knowing he'd coerced her into joining him for that drink. He'd wanted it to be her choice, her terms, her desire.

It was almost comical, how this conservative art history pro-fessor had gotten under his skin. She was so different from the women he'd dated in the past. Smarter, prettier, more serious, definitely more pigheaded. She annoyed him; she excited him; she made him laugh. He knew he should just let her go since she obviously didn't want to pursue a relationship, but his in-stincts kept screaming for him not to let her out of his sight, that if he blinked, she'd be gone, and someone very important would be slipping through his grasp. It made no sense to him, and yet he'd always trusted his instincts. They'd never failed him before.

He kicked a pebble on his way to the car, feeling like kicking something harder than a rock. His own thick skull, perhaps.

He pressed a button on the remote to unlock the doors, then swore when he realized his wrist was bare. Shoot. He must have left his watch back at the practice arena. He always seemed to misplace the damn thing. He hated wearing a watch to begin with, but it had been a gift from his parents in honor of his first professional game eight years ago. Chris and Jane Croft were ferociously proud of their son, and he witnessed that pride every time he went back to Michigan for a visit and saw them staring at that watch.

Sighing, he turned around and headed back to the entrance of the sprawling gray building. The Warriors practiced in a private arena a few miles from the Lincoln Center, a little unorthodox but Brody found it somewhat of a relief. It meant the media never filmed their practices, which took the pressure off the players to always be on top of their game.

The double doors at the entrance led to a large sterile lobby. A blue door to the right opened onto the rink. To the left were the hallways leading to the locker rooms, and when Brody strode into the arena he immediately noticed the two people huddled by the locker-room corridor. Their backs were turned, and Brody quickly sidestepped to the right, ducking into another hall that featured a row of vending machines.

"You shouldn't have come here," came Craig Wyatt's somber voice.

Brody sucked in a breath, hoping the Warriors captain and his companion hadn't spotted him.

He'd sure as hell spotted them, though.

Which posed the question: what was Craig Wyatt doing whispering with Sheila Houston?

"I know. I just had to see you," Sheila said, her voice so

soft Brody had to strain his ears to hear her. "That meeting with the lawyers today was terrible…" There was a faint sob.

"Shh, it's okay, baby."

Baby?

Deciding he'd officially heard enough—and that he'd return for his watch another time—Brody edged toward the emergency exit at the end of the hallway. He turned the door handle, praying an alarm wouldn't go off. It didn't. Relieved, he exited the side door of the building and practically sprinted back to his car.

The drive to his Hyde Park home brought with it a tornado of confusion that made his head spin. Craig Wyatt and Sheila Houston? The player rumored to be having an affair with the owner's wife was *Wyatt?* Brody would've never expected it from the straight-laced Mr. Serious.

If it was true, then that meant the idea of bribes exchanging hands in the franchise might not be a lie after all. Craig Wyatt might have the personality of a brick wall, but he was the captain of the team, as well as the eyes and ears. He frequently kept track of everyone's progress, making sure they were all in tip-top shape and focused on the game. If he suspected anyone had taken a bribe, he would've investigated it, no doubt about it.

Jeez, was Wyatt the source Sheila had referred to in that interview? Had he been the one to tell her about the bribes?

Or…

Shit, had Wyatt taken a bribe himself? No, that didn't make sense. Sheila wouldn't draw attention to the bribery and illegal betting if her lover was one of the guilty parties.

Brody steered into his driveway and killed the engine. He reached up and pinched the bridge of his nose, hoping to ward off an oncoming headache.

Damn. This was not good at all.

He didn't particularly care what or who Craig Wyatt did

in his spare time, but if Wyatt knew something about these rumors…

Maybe he should just confront the man, flat out ask what he knew. Or maybe he'd ask Becker to do it for him. Becker was good at stuff like that, knew how to handle tough situations and still keep a clear head.

He rubbed his temples, then leaned his forehead against the steering wheel for a moment. Lord, he didn't want to deal with any of this. If he had his way, this entire scandal would just disappear; he'd play out the rest of the season then resign with the Warriors or sign with a new team. His career would be secure and his life would be peachy.

And Hayden Houston would be right back in his bed. A guy could dream, after all.

"I WILL NOT WATCH porn," Hayden muttered to herself later that night, stepping out of the enormous marble bathtub in the master suite of the penthouse. She reached for the terry-cloth robe hanging behind the door, slipped it on and tightened the sash around her waist.

Not that there was anything wrong with porn. She wasn't a nun, after all—she'd watched a few X-rated videos in her twenty-six years. But she'd never used porn to get over a man before, and besides, she'd had six orgasms in two days. She should be thoroughly exhausted by now and not thinking about having sex at all.

Unfortunately, she *was* thinking about sex, and it was all Brody Croft's fault.

At dinner, Darcy had again pointed out that a fling wouldn't be the end of the world, but Hayden still wasn't sold on the idea. She got the feeling that if she gave Brody an inch, he'd take a mile. That if she suggested a fling, he'd show up with an engagement ring.

Barefoot, she stepped out of the bathroom into the master bedroom, pushing wet hair out of her eyes. She'd finally gotten around to unpacking her suitcase this morning, but the suite's huge walk-in closet still looked empty. She changed into a pair of thin gray sweatpants and a cotton tank top, brushed her hair and tied it into a ponytail, then headed for the kitchen.

Normally she hated hotels, but her father's penthouse at the Ritz-Carlton surpassed any ordinary hotel suite. He'd lived here before marrying Sheila, and the apartment had everything Hayden could possibly need, including a large kitchen that was fully stocked and surprisingly cozy. It reminded her of her kitchen back home, making her homesick for the West Coast. In San Francisco, she hadn't needed to worry about anything except how she was going to get her boyfriend into bed.

Here, she had her father's problems, her stepmother's lies and Brody Croft's incessant attempts to get *her* into bed.

Quit thinking about Brody.

Right. He was definitely on tonight's don't-think-about list.

After she'd made a bowl of popcorn and brewed herself a cup of green tea, she got comfortable on one of the leather couches in the living area and switched on the TV. She was totally ready to lose herself in that van Gogh biography. Since she was teaching an entire course on him next semester, she figured she ought to get reacquainted with the guy.

She scrolled through the channels, searching for the program, but couldn't seem to find it. The Biography Channel was telling the life story of a Hollywood actress who'd just been busted on cocaine charges. The History Channel featured a show on the Civil War. She kept scrolling. No van Gogh to be seen.

Great. Just freaking great. Could nothing go right in her life? All she'd wanted to do tonight was watch a show about her favorite artist and not think about Brody Croft. Was that really too much to ask?

Apparently so.

She skipped past a shocking number of reality shows, finally stopping on the Discovery Channel, which was playing a special on sharks. She sighed in resignation and settled the bowl of popcorn in her lap.

"The great white shark can smell one drop of blood in twenty-five gallons of water," came a monotone voice.

Hayden popped a few kernels in her mouth and chewed thoughtfully, watching as a lethal-looking shark swam across the screen.

"The great white does not chew his food. Rather, he takes massive bites and swallows the pieces whole."

Yeah, like Brody… *No Brody thoughts allowed, missy.*

"There have been reports of great whites exceeding twenty feet in length. They can weigh in at over seven thousand pounds."

Ten minutes and fifteen shark facts later, Hayden was stretching out her legs and wiggling her toes, wondering if she should apply some red nail polish. This shark documentary was getting old.

She pressed the guide button on the remote control, scrolled down, skipped the barrage of sports channels, stopped briefly on CNN, then scrolled again. She saw a listing for something called *The Secretary* and decided to click on it, but what came on the screen wasn't the sitcom her students at Berkeley were always raving about.

It was, of course, porn.

"You're a very fast typist, Betty."

"Thank you, Mr. Larson. My fingers have always been my biggest asset."

"I bet they have. Bring your hand a little closer."

"Ooh, Mr. Larson, that tickles."

"Do you like it?"

"Mmm, yes."

"What about this?"

"Mmm, even better."

Hayden had to bite her lip to refrain from bursting into laughter. On the screen, Betty and her boss began making out. Mr. Larsen's big hairy hand disappeared under Betty's conservative skirt. Loud moaning ensued.

She shook her head and pressed a button on the remote. Betty and Mr. Larson disappeared, replaced by a great white shark.

You want me, come and get me.

The sound of Brody's sandpaper-rough voice filled her head. She let out a long breath, exasperated. Why couldn't she stop thinking about the guy? And why couldn't she stop wanting him? She wanted him so badly she could practically feel those big muscular arms around her waist.

But sometimes the things you wanted weren't necessarily the ones you needed.

At the moment, she needed to concentrate on supporting her dad through his divorce and maybe finally call Doug back to tell him she'd slept with someone else and that it was time to turn their break into a breakup.

But what she *wanted* was one more night with Brody Croft.

It doesn't have to be black and white.

She sat there for a moment, chewing on her lower lip as Darcy's words buzzed around in her brain.

Was her friend right? Was she overanalyzing all of this? She'd always had the tendency to pick and prod at each situation until she'd sucked every last drop of fun or enjoyment from it. This wasn't an art history lecture she needed to plan for—it was just sex. Was there really anything wrong with delving into that gray area and enjoying a carnal ride with a man she found wildly attractive?

She turned off the television and reached for the phone.

6

THE CALL FROM HAYDEN came as a total shock. Brody had just stepped out of the shower, where he'd stood under the hot spray for a good half hour to get the kinks out of his muscles. He'd intended to grab a beer from the fridge and watch the highlight reel on ESPN, maybe give Becker a call to talk about Craig Wyatt, and then his cell phone began chirping out a tinny rendition of Beethoven's Symphony No. 9 and Hayden's throaty voice was on the other end.

Come over.

She'd only spoken those two words, then disconnected, leaving him both pleased and befuddled.

Obviously she'd finally changed her mind and taken him up on his offer to continue the fantasy she'd started two nights ago, but was it still just sex she craved? Or was she looking for something extra this time around?

Shit, he was getting ahead of himself here. Hayden was simply inviting him back into her bed for another wild romp, not offering to make a commitment.

He quickly put on a pair of jeans and pulled an old Warriors jersey over his head. Then he grabbed his car keys from the credenza in the hallway, shoved his wallet into his back pocket and left the house, breathing in the damp night air.

It was mid-May, which meant the nights were still cool and the chance of a thunderstorm or even a freak blizzard wasn't all that far-fetched, but Brody loved this time of year, when spring and summer battled for domination over Chicago's climate. He'd lived in this city almost eight years now, and he'd grown to appreciate and enjoy everything about it, even the indecisive seasons.

When he pulled up in front of Hayden's hotel, a light drizzle of rain was sliding across the windshield. He hopped out of the SUV and entered the lobby just as a bolt of lightning filled the sky. Thunder roared ominously in the distance, growing louder and louder until the rain became a steady downpour.

Shaking droplets of water from his hair, he approached the check-in desk and asked the clerk behind it to ring Hayden's suite. A moment later, the clerk walked him over to the elevator and inserted a key into the panel that would allow Brody access to the penthouse, then left him alone in the car.

The elevator soared upward, its doors opening into the suite, where Hayden was waiting for him.

"I have some ground rules," she said in lieu of a greeting.

He grinned. "Hello to you, too."

"Hello. I have some ground rules."

He tossed his car keys on a glass table beside one of the couches and moved toward her.

Even in sweats, she looked amazing. He liked how she'd pulled her hair back in a messy ponytail, how a few haphazard strands framed her face, which was devoid of makeup. He especially liked how her thin tank top didn't hide the fact that she wore no bra.

His mouth ran dry as he dragged his gaze across those gorgeous breasts, the outline of her dusky nipples visible through the white shirt.

Her fair cheeks grew flushed at his perusal. "Don't ogle. It's unbecoming."

He grinned. "Ah, I was wondering where Miss Prim and Proper had gone. Hello, Professor, nice to see you again."

"I am *not* prim and proper," she protested.

"Not in bed anyway…"

"Ground rules," she repeated firmly.

He released a sigh. "All right. Get it out of your system."

She leaned against the arm of the couch, resting her hands on her thighs. "This is only going to be sex," she began, her throaty voice wavering in a way that brought a smile to his lips. "Continuing the fantasy, or whatever it was you said. Agreed?"

"I'm not agreeing to anything yet. Is there more?"

"My father can't know anything about it." She paused, looking uncomfortable. "And I'd prefer if we weren't seen in public together."

His nostrils flared. "Ashamed of being linked to a hockey player?"

"Look, you already know the franchise is taking some heat, Brody. I don't want to make things worse for my dad by giving the media more fuel for the fire they're determined to start."

He had to admit her words made sense. After seeing Craig Wyatt whispering with Sheila Houston at the arena today, Brody had no interest in stoking the fire. Best-case scenario, if he was spotted with Hayden, the press would sensationalize the relationship the way they were currently sensationalizing everything else associated with the Warriors. Worst-case scenario, a jerk reporter would insinuate that the team owner's daughter knew of her father's guilt and was either trying to shut Brody up because he was involved, or sleeping with him to find out what he knew.

He didn't particularly like either of those scenarios.

Still, he wasn't about to let Hayden get her way entirely. He had a few demands himself.

"If I agree to your rules, you have to agree to mine," he said roughly, crossing his arms over his chest.

She swallowed. "Like what?"

"If you're in my bed, that's the only bed you'll be in." He set his jaw. "I won't share you, especially not with the guy waiting for you in California."

"Of course."

"And you have to promise to keep an open mind."

Interest flickered in her gaze. "Sexually?"

"Sure. But emotionally, too. All I'm saying is that if things between us get…deeper, you can't run away from it."

After a beat of silence, she nodded. "I can do that. And do you agree to keep whatever we do here to yourself?"

"I can do that," he mimicked with a grin.

"Then what are you waiting for?" she asked. "Take off your clothes already."

HAYDEN COULD barely contain her amusement as Brody pulled his jersey over his head and tossed it aside. He reminded her of a kid on Christmas morning. The eagerness practically radiated from his tall, powerful body, but when he pushed his jeans down his legs there was nothing comical about the situation anymore.

His cock sprang up against the material of his boxers, demanding attention and making Hayden's mouth grow dry.

No matter how unsettling she found Brody's terms, it was too late to reverse her decision. He wanted her to keep an open mind, fine. But she highly doubted things between them would get *deeper*, as he'd suggested. Their one-night stand may have turned into a fling, but she was confident it wouldn't go further than that.

Besides, right now she didn't want or need to think about the future, not when there were more important things to focus on. Such as Brody's spectacular body and all the things she wanted to do to it.

An impish grin lifted the corner of her mouth as she remembered what he'd done to *her* body the night before at the bar. Her next move suddenly became very clear.

"The keeping-an-open-mind part," she said mischievously. "It goes for you, too, right?"

Brody kicked aside his boxers and fixed her with an intrigued stare. "What do you have in mind?"

She didn't answer. Crooking her finger at him, she gestured for him to follow her down the hallway. They entered the bedroom, where she turned her finger to the bed and said, "Get comfortable."

Brody raised his brows. "Are you planning to join me?"

"Eventually."

He lowered himself onto the bed and leaned against the mountain of pillows at the headboard.

Fighting a smile, Hayden swept her gaze over Brody's long naked body sprawled before her.

"I'm feeling lonely," he murmured. "Are you going to stand there all night and watch me?"

"Maybe."

"What'll it take to get you to come here?"

She chewed on the inside of her cheek, thoughtful. "I don't know. You'd have to make it worth my while, give me a good reason to get into that bed with you."

He chuckled and grasped his shaft with his hand. "This isn't reason enough?"

She laughed. "God, you're arrogant." She stared at his erection, the way his fingers had curled around the base, and moisture gathered in her panties. There was something seriously enticing about watching this man touch himself.

"C'mere," he cajoled. "You don't really want to make me do this alone, do you?"

His gruff voice sent shivers through her, making her nipples poke against her tank top. "I don't know," she said again. "I'm getting pretty turned-on watching you right now…"

Still watching his hand, she strode toward the desk under the curtained window, pulled the chair out and lowered herself on it. "Tell me what you'd want me to do, if I was lying there with you."

Something raw and powerful flashed in his smoky blue eyes. "I think you already know."

"Humor me."

A hint of a smile lifted one corner of his mouth. Without breaking eye contact, he moved his hand up his shaft. From where she sat she could see a bead of moisture at the tip. Her sex throbbed.

"Well, I'd definitely encourage you to bring your tongue into play," he said, his voice lowering to a husky pitch.

He squeezed his erection.

Uncontrollable need raced through her body and settled between her legs.

"Some licking would have to be involved," he continued, propping one hand behind his head while his other hand continued stroking. "Sucking, of course."

"Of course," she agreed, shocked by the pure lust resonating through her.

Brody shot her a wolfish look.

She gasped when he quickened his pace. No man had ever done that in front of her before, and the sexual heat pulsating through her body was so strong she could barely breathe. There was something so kinky, so *dirty* about the way he was lying there, stroking himself while she watched. And that she was still fully clothed only made the situation hotter. It gave her the upper hand, reminding her of a fantasy she hadn't dared to think about in years. Scratch that—she'd thought about it only yesterday, when she'd seen Brody at the arena.

She licked her lips, debating whether or not to bring it up. "What are you thinking about?"

She was certain her embarrassment was written all over her face. And yet the pang of embarrassment was accompanied by a jolt of excitement, because for the first time in her life she was thinking about making that particular fantasy come true.

"Hayden?"

He stopped stroking and she almost cried out in disappointment. "No, keep doing that," she murmured, meeting his eyes again.

"Not until you tell me what's on your mind."

"I…you'll probably think it's silly."

"Try me."

She couldn't believe she was considering confessing her deepest, darkest fantasy to a man she'd known less than a week when she'd never raised the subject around guys she'd dated for months. That in itself said a lot.

Try him.

She swallowed and got to her feet. Eyeing her expectantly, Brody let go of his shaft and leaned his head against both hands, waiting. "Well?" he prompted.

"Promise not to laugh?"

"I won't laugh. Scout's honor." He held up his fingers in a sign that she was fairly certain did *not* belong to the Boy Scouts, but, hell, at least he'd promised.

She took a breath, held it, then released it at the same time she blurted out the words. "I've always wanted to tie a man to my bed."

He laughed softly.

"Hey!" Heat seared her cheeks. "You promised."

"I'm not laughing at the request," he said quickly. "You just took me by surprise."

Relief washed over her, dimming her humiliation. "You're not freaked?"

"Nope. I'm too turned-on to be freaked."

Her focus dropped to his groin, which confirmed his admission. He was thick and hard, a sight that caused every last drop of hesitation and embarrassment to drain from her body like water from a tub. That spot between her legs began to ache, pushing her to action.

"Keep your arms just like that," she ordered, drifting toward the walk-in closet. She grabbed what she needed from the top drawer of the built-in dresser and sauntered over to the bed.

Brody looked at the sheer panty hose in her hands and he grinned. "No fuzzy pink handcuffs?"

"Sorry, I left them in California."

"Pity."

Laughing, she looped the panty hose around his wrists, brushing her fingers over the calluses on his palm. His hands were so strong, fingers long and tapered. A thrill shot through her as she tied those sturdy hands to the headboard. That he let her do it, without moving, without complaining, only deepened the thrill.

She liked it, this feeling of control, something she'd never really felt in the bedroom before. She was all about control when it came to her life, her job, her goals. But sex? Not so much.

With Brody, she was discovering a part of herself she'd denied for a long time. That first night when she'd propositioned him, then letting him touch her in a public bar, now tying him up to her bed—how on earth had he managed to unleash this passionate side of her?

"So what now?" he said hoarsely. "How does this bondage fantasy of yours play out?"

"Well, the fantasy includes some payback actually." She made sure his hands were secure, then straddled him, still fully clothed. "You tortured me last night, Brody."

"You seemed to enjoy it," he teased.

"But you enjoyed it, too, didn't you? You loved having that control over me, driving me wild with your fingers and knowing I wasn't going to fight it." She arched one slim eyebrow. "It's my turn."

He tested the bindings. The headboard shook. "I could easily get out of this position, you know."

"But you won't."

"You sound sure of that."

She bent down and pressed a kiss to his jaw, then licked her way to his earlobe and bit it. He shuddered, his cock jutting against her pelvis. "You're dying for it," she mocked.

A crooked smile stretched across his mouth. "Do people out on the West Coast know how deliciously evil you are, Hayden?"

"They don't have a clue," she said with a self-deprecating sigh.

He threw his head back and laughed. The desire and awe dancing in his eyes sent a wave of confidence rushing through her. Brody made her feel that she could do anything she wanted, be anyone she wanted, confess to any naughty longing she wanted, and he wouldn't judge her.

"Well, it's your turn, as you said," Brody told her. "Let's see what you've got. I warn you, I don't lose control easily."

"We'll see about that."

She pressed both palms to his chest, relishing the hard feel of him, running her fingers through the light sprinkling of hair covering his golden skin. Dipping her head, she traced his collarbone with her tongue.

Brody chuckled. "You can do better than that."

She narrowed her eyes. Was he really convinced he could

stay in control? Arrogant man! She'd just have to show him, wouldn't she?

Not rising to his bait, she bent down and covered one flat nipple with her mouth.

He drew in a breath.

She ran her tongue down his chest, scraping her nails along his skin. He tasted like heaven—salty, spicy, masculine—and the hair leading to his groin tickled her lips as she kissed her way south. Her mouth finally reached his erection, but she made no move to wrap her lips around it. Instead she gently flicked her tongue against his tip then blew a stream of air over the moisture she'd left there.

Brody jerked and let out a soft curse.

"Everything okay?" she asked politely, lifting her head just in time to see the arousal creasing his rugged features.

"Is that all you've got?" he groaned.

"On the contrary." She licked her lips and sent him a heavy-lidded look. "I'm just getting started."

Oh, boy, there was nothing more empowering than driving a man as *manly* as Brody Croft into sheer and total orgasmic oblivion. Flames of arousal and satisfaction licked through Hayden's body as she circled the tip of Brody's cock with her tongue, savoring the taste of him.

Curling her fingers around his shaft, she licked him again, then sucked him into her mouth, trying not to smile when he released a low moan of pleasure. God, why hadn't she done this before? She wanted to berate herself for everything she'd been missing.

In the back of her mind a little voice suggested that perhaps she'd never admitted this fantasy because she hadn't found the right man to admit it to, but she forced the voice and its unsettling implications out of her brain. No more thinking. She didn't want to analyze anything about this.

She moved her mouth up and down his shaft, and when she reached one hand down to cup his balls, he shuddered and grew even harder. Her mind was spinning from the incredible feel of him against her lips.

Lightly stroking his rock-hard thigh, she kissed his sensitive underside, then pumped him with her hand while she took him deep in her mouth again.

"You're evil," he wheezed out.

She lifted her head. "What happened to the master of control?"

"He didn't stand a chance."

She laughed. With one final kiss to his tip, she moved up to straddle him. She could feel the heat of his naked body searing through her clothing, making her pants feel like a tight, hot nuisance. But she didn't undress. Not yet.

Leaning forward, she pressed her lips to his and deepened the kiss. He made a frustrated sound and yet again tugged at the bindings constricting his hands. He was right—one forceful tug and the knots would come apart—but he continued lying there at her mercy. His biceps flexed as he tested the knots again. He let out a soft curse.

"Damn it, Hayden, I need to touch you."

"Touch? Nope, sorry."

She lifted her tank top over her head and threw it aside, baring her breasts. "But I'll let you taste." Bending closer, she offered him a sampling, and drew in a breath when he captured one nipple in his mouth and began feasting. He sucked on the rigid bud, hard, biting it gently until she cried out with pleasure that teetered toward pain.

"More," he rasped, pulling away and staring at her pleadingly.

She laughed. "Define more."

His gaze lowered to her thighs, a clear message of what he

desired, and her sex instantly throbbed in response. If she gave him what he wanted, what *she* wanted, then the domination game would be shot to hell…but did she really care at this point? Could she last one more second without having this man's hands all over her?

The moisture between her legs provided the answer to that question—a big fat no.

As he inched down a little, so that his head was flat on the pillow, she quickly slipped out of her pants, tore off her panties and knelt over him.

His tongue darted out and flicked over her clit.

"Oh," she moaned, nearly falling backward at the jolt of excitement that ran through her. She was closer than she'd thought. The rippling wave of pleasure swelling inside her confirmed that she was on the brink, her orgasm about to crash to the surface.

Her thighs trembled as she tried to move away from his probing tongue, but he wouldn't let her.

"I want you to come in my mouth," he murmured, the husky sound reverberating against her flesh.

She reached for the headboard, gripped his bound hands and twined her fingers with his. Her heart thumped, her knees shook, and the moment she leaned into his warm lips again, the second he suckled her clit, she exploded.

Her climax tore through her, fierce, reckless. She gasped, sucking in oxygen as shards of colorful light danced before her eyes and prickled her flushed skin. Still shaking, she sagged against the headboard, struggling to regain her sense of equilibrium while she fumbled with the knots on his hands.

"I need you inside me. Now," she squeezed out, finally untying him.

With a grin, he rotated his wrists to get the blood flowing

again, but made no move to flip her over and plunge into her as she'd requested. "It's your show, remember?"

He curled his fingers around her waist and pushed her down so she was straddling him again. From the end table, he swiped a condom she hadn't even noticed him bring into the bedroom and handed it to her. "Do with me what you please."

Swallowing, she rolled the condom onto his erection and shifted her legs. She was wet and ready for him, more than ready, but she didn't guide him inside her. Instead, she brushed her nipples over his chest, enjoying the way his eyes narrowed with pleasure.

She ground her pelvis against him, teased him by pushing against his tip and then edging away from it. Feeling bold and wanton, she leaned forward, let her breasts graze his mouth, and murmured, "Tell me what you want, Brody."

His voice hoarse, he said, "You."

"Me what?"

A wicked gleam flashed in his eyes. "What was it you said to me that first night? Oh, right. I want you to fuck me."

Oh, my.

Without another word, she lowered herself onto him, taking him all the way in, and began to ride him. The pleasure cascading through her body was almost too much to bear. He felt so good inside, so right and perfect.

She increased her pace, moving over him faster, harder, his husky groans urging her on.

He lifted his lean hips and met her thrust for thrust. Then he grasped her ass and rolled her over, his powerful body covering hers as he drove into her. *Yes.* Her insides clenched, pleading with her for release.

"Will you come for me?" he murmured, slowing his pace.

She made an unintelligible sound.

He chuckled. "What was that?"

"Yes," she choked out.

With a satisfied nod, he plunged into her, hard, rough, stealing the breath right of her lungs. He reached down and stroked the place where they joined, continuing to pump inside her until she finally exploded again.

She gave herself to the orgasm that raced through her body. In the heavenly haze she heard Brody's deep groan, felt his fingers dig into her hips as he jerked inside her.

Struggling to steady her breathing, she ran her hands up and down his sweat-soaked back, enjoying the hard planes and defined muscles under her fingertips. "God, that was…" She trailed off.

He touched her chin, lightly dragging his thumbnail over her jaw. "That was what?"

"Incredible." A laugh flew out. "And to think I was going to spend the evening watching a documentary on a guy who cut his own ear off."

7

"LET'S ORDER room service," Brody said a few minutes later, slipping his boxers on.

He watched as Hayden put on her tank top and then attempted to fix the ponytail that had seen better days. Wayward strands of hair fell into her eyes and he smiled at the knowledge that her disheveled state was the result of rolling around in bed with him. She looked rumpled and beautiful and so damn cute he marched over and planted a kiss on her lips. She tasted of toothpaste and popcorn and something uniquely Hayden.

With a little whimper, she pulled his head closer and sank into the kiss, flicking her tongue against his in a tantalizing way that made him hard again.

Just as he lowered his hands to her breasts, she pushed him back. "What happened to room service?" she teased.

"Screw it."

"Knock yourself out. I, for one, am starved." With a grin, she brushed past him and left the bedroom.

He stared down at the erection poking against his boxers. Damn, how did this woman turn him on so fiercely? He felt like a horny teenager again.

He put on his jeans, used the washroom then drifted toward the living room.

"How do cheeseburgers sound?" she called when she spotted him lingering in the hallway.

His stomach growled with approval. "Great."

He joined her on the couch. As she dialed room service and placed their order, he noticed a stack of papers sitting on the table. Curious, he leaned forward and examined the first sheet. It looked like a biography on Rembrandt, neatly typed. The margins were full of handwritten notes.

"What's this?" he asked when she'd hung up the phone.

"Ideas for the Color Theory class I'm teaching in the fall. I plan to focus on Rembrandt for a few lectures."

"Rembrandt, huh? I thought all of his paintings were pretty dark and foreboding." The snippet of information stored in his brain came as a surprise to him. He hadn't thought he'd paid any attention during art history class his senior year of high school.

Hayden also looked surprised, but pleased. "Actually, that's what I want to focus on, the misconceptions about certain artists and their use of color. Did you know that Rembrandt's *Night Watch* is in fact a day scene?"

A vague image of the painting surfaced in his mind. "I remember it being very dark."

"It was—until the painting was cleaned." She grinned. "The canvas was coated with loads of varnish. When it was removed, it turned out to be daylight. A lot of his paintings ended up looking very different once they were cleaned or restored, proving that he definitely knew what he was doing when it came to color."

She grew more animated as she hurried on. "Same with Michelangelo. People didn't view him as much of a colorist, but when the Sistine Chapel was cleaned, it was so vivid, the colors so vibrant, that everyone was shocked."

"I never knew that."

"It took longer to clean that ceiling than it did to paint it," she added. "It was covered in so much soot and dirt that when they were removed the entire scene looked different. That's one of the things I want to talk to my students about, how something as simple as cleaning or restoring can change your entire view of a piece of art."

He nodded. "Sort of like when the Zamboni cleans the ice during second period intermission. Changes the entire playing surface."

He saw her mouth quirk and suspected she was trying not to laugh. "Yeah. I guess there's a similarity there."

Setting down the papers, he said, "You're really into art, huh?"

"Of course. It's my passion."

A smile reached his lips. He hadn't spent much time with women who were passionate about anything outside the bedroom, and the light in Hayden's green eyes tugged at something inside him. He realized this was the first time she'd opened up to him, engaged in a conversation that didn't include ground rules, and he liked it.

"So do you paint, or just lecture about painters?" he asked.

"I used to draw and paint a lot when I was younger, but not so much anymore."

"How come?"

She shrugged. "I was always more fascinated with other people's work than with my own. My undergrad was mostly studio work, but I did my master's in art history. I discovered I liked studying great artists better than trying to become one myself." She drew her knees up into a cross-legged position and asked, "What did you study in college?"

"Sports sciences," he answered. "You know, kinesiology, sports medicine. And I minored in athletic coaching."

"Seriously?"

He didn't respond. Her expression revealed nothing, but he got the feeling she didn't believe him, which made him feel like he was in high school all over again. The kid who'd been written off by his teachers as a big dumb oaf just because he happened to be good at sports. They'd stuck the jock label on him, and no matter how hard he'd tried to tear it off, the judgmental attitudes remained intact. One time he'd even been accused of cheating on an English test he'd spent hours studying for, all because his teacher had decided that a kid who spent all his time handling a puck couldn't possibly finish a book like *Crime and Punishment*.

Hayden must have sensed his irritation because she quickly added, "I believe you. It's just…well, most of the athletes I knew growing up only went to college for the athletic scholarship and just skipped all the academic classes."

"My parents would have killed me if I'd skipped class," he said, rolling his eyes. "They only allowed me to play hockey if I maintained an A average."

Hayden looked impressed. "What do your parents do for a living?"

"Dad's a mechanic, and Mom works in a hair salon." He paused. "Money was always tight during my childhood." He resisted the urge to glance around the lavish penthouse, which was an obvious sign that Hayden hadn't had the same problem growing up.

He wasn't quite sure why he'd brought up that money part, either. He hated talking about his childhood. Hated thinking about it, too. As much as he loved his parents, he didn't like to be reminded of how hard life had been to them. How his mom used to stay up at night clipping coupons and how his dad walked to work—even when Michigan's winter was at its worst—each time their beat-up Chevy truck broke down. Fortunately, his parents would never have to worry about money again, thanks to his lucrative career.

The phone rang, putting an end to their conversation.

Hayden picked up the receiver, then hung up and said room service was on its way.

As Hayden headed for the elevator to greet the bellhop with the cart, Brody turned on the television, flipped through a few channels, then finally stopped on the eleven-o'clock news.

Rolling the cart into the living room, Hayden uncovered their food and placed a plate in front of him. The aroma of French fries and ground beef floated toward him, making his mouth water. Funny, he hadn't even noticed how hungry he was when Hayden had had him tied to her bed. He'd been satisfying a different sort of appetite then.

He'd just taken a big bite of his cheeseburger when a familiar face flashed across the plasma screen. He nearly choked on the burger, as a wave of unease washed over him. Hayden had also noticed her father's image on the TV, and she quickly grabbed the remote to turn up the volume. They caught the Channel 8 newscaster in midsentence.

"—came forward this afternoon and admitted there is truth to the rumors surrounding the Chicago Warriors franchise. The player, who refused to be named, claims that the bribery and illegal betting activities Warriors owner Presley Houston is accused of are in fact true."

Brody suppressed a groan. Next to him, Hayden made a startled little sound.

"An hour ago, the league announced they will be launching a full investigation into these allegations."

The newscaster went on to recap the accusation that Presley had bribed players to throw at least two games, and that he'd placed bets on the outcomes. The divorce was also mentioned, as well as Sheila Houston's alleged affair with a Warrior, but by that point Brody had tuned out the news segment.

Who had come forward? It couldn't be Becker, because his friend would've called him with a heads-up before he did anything like that. Yeah, Becker would've definitely warned him.

Craig Wyatt, though, seemed like a likely candidate, especially after what Brody had witnessed at the arena earlier today. The reporters had been pretty rough on Sheila Houston, many of them holding the firm belief that she was lying. It made sense that Wyatt would step in and try to support the woman in his bed.

The headache Brody had tried to ignore before came back with full force. He reached up to rub his throbbing temples. Damn. He wished he knew which one of his teammates had confessed. Whoever it was, this probably didn't bode well for tomorrow's game. How would anybody be able to focus with a possible criminal investigation hanging over their heads?

"It's not true."

Hayden's soft voice jarred him from his thoughts, and he glanced over to see her big eyes pleading with him. "Right?" she said wearily. "It's not true."

"I don't know." He raked a hand through his hair, then absently picked up a French fry. Not that he had an appetite anymore. That news report had destroyed any desire he had for food. He dropped the fry and looked back at Hayden, who seemed to be waiting expectantly for him to continue. "I really don't know, babe. So far, there's been no proof that Pres bribed anyone."

"So far. But if that report we saw just now is true…"

Her breath hitched, and her pained expression tore at his heart.

"Were you… Did he…" She sounded tortured, as if saying each word took great effort. "Did he offer you a bribe?" she finally asked.

"Absolutely not."

"But he could have bribed someone else, another player."

"He could have," Brody said guardedly.

She grew silent, looking so achingly sad that he reached over to draw her into his arms. Her hair tickled his chin, the sweet scent of her wafting into his nose. He wanted to kiss her, to make love to her again, but it was totally not the time. She was upset, and the way she pressed her head into the crook of his neck and snuggled closer told him she needed comfort at the moment, not sex.

"God, this is such a mess," she murmured, her breath warming his skin. "Dad is already stressed-out because of the divorce, and now…"

She abruptly lifted her head, her lips set in a tight line. "I refuse to believe he did what they're accusing him of. My dad is a lot of things, but he's not a criminal."

The certainty in her eyes was unmistakable, and Brody wisely kept quiet. He'd always admired and respected Presley Houston, but experience had taught him that even people you admired and respected could screw up.

"Whoever came forward has to be lying," Hayden said firmly. She swallowed. "This will all get cleared up during the investigation. It has to."

She slid close to him again. "I don't want to think about this anymore. Can we just pretend we didn't see that newscast?" Without waiting for an answer, she went on. "And while we're at it, we can pretend I came home for a vacation rather than to deal with my father's problems." She sighed against his shoulder. "God, a vacation would be so good. I could really use some fun right now."

He smoothed her hair, loving how soft it felt under his fingers. "What did you have in mind?"

She tilted her head up and smiled. "We could go see a movie tomorrow—it's been ages since I've been to the movies. Or we could walk along the waterfront, go to Navy Pier. I don't know, just have fun, damn it!"

As much as he hated disappointing her, Brody smiled gently and said, "I would love to, but I can't. The team's catching a plane to L.A. at 9:00 a.m. There's a game tomorrow night."

The light drained out of her eyes, but she gave him a quick smile as if to hide her reaction. "Oh. Right. Dad mentioned something about an away game."

His arms felt empty as she disentangled herself from the embrace and inched back, absently reaching for a French fry on her plate. She popped it into her mouth, chewing slowly, not looking at him.

"How about Sunday?" he suggested, anxious to make things right and at the same time not sure what he'd done wrong.

"I have this party to go to." She pushed her plate away, apparently as uninterested in eating as he was. "It's important to my dad."

"Then another time," he said. "I promise you, I'll take you out and give you the fun you need."

Her expression grew strained. "It's okay, Brody. You don't have to indulge me. It's probably a silly idea to go out on a date anyway."

He bristled. "Why is it silly?"

She blew out an exasperated breath. "This is only supposed to be a fling. Playing out a few sexual fantasies."

A fling. Something inside him hardened at the word. Casual flings had pretty much been his entire life for the past ten years, serious relationships never even making a blip on his radar. And then he'd met Hayden and suddenly he wasn't thinking about casual anymore. He liked her. A lot. Hell, he'd actually experienced a flicker of excitement when she'd mentioned engaging in normal couple things like going to the movies or walking by the lake. He'd never felt the urge to do stuff like that with the previous women in his life. He hadn't cared enough, and that would have sounded awful if not for the fact that they hadn't cared, either.

Crazy as it was, Hayden was the first woman, aside from a reporter, who'd ever asked him about his parents or his college major. Mundane little questions that people asked each other all the time, and yet something he'd been lacking.

He'd seen the potential when Hayden had first walked up to him in that bar. Somehow, he'd known deep down that this was a woman he could have a meaningful relationship with.

And it was damn ironic that she only wanted a goddamn fling.

"What happened to promising to keep an open mind?" he asked quietly.

"I plan on keeping that promise." She shifted her gaze. "But you can't blame me for being skeptical about this becoming anything deeper."

"You don't think it will?"

"Honestly?" She looked him square in the eye. "No, I don't."

He frowned. "You sound convinced of that."

"I am." Pushing an errant strand of hair from her eyes, she shrugged. "I'm going back to the West Coast in a couple of months, and even if I were staying here, our lives don't mesh."

Irritation swelled inside him. "How do you figure that?"

"You're a hockey player. I'm a professor."

"So?"

"So, our careers alone tell me how different we are. I've lived in your world, Brody. I grew up in it. Dad and I had most of our conversations on airplanes on the way to whatever city his team was playing against. I lived in five states during a fifteen-year period. And I hated it."

"Your father was a hockey coach," he pointed out.

"And the travel requirements are not much different for

players. I had no say in the career my father chose for himself. But when it comes to what I want in a partner, I can choose."

"The guy in San Francisco, what does he do?"

Her discomfort at discussing the guy who Brody now thought of as the Other Man was evident as she began to fidget with her hands. She laced her fingers together, unlaced them, then tapped them against her thighs. "Actually, he teaches art history at Berkeley, too."

How frickin' peachy. "What else?" he demanded.

She faltered. "What do you mean?"

"So you're both interested in art. What else makes this relationship so delightfully rewarding?"

He almost winced at the sarcasm he heard in his tone. Damn it, he was acting like a total ass here, and from the cloudy look in Hayden's eyes, she obviously thought the same thing.

"My relationship with Doug is none of your concern. I promised to remain sexually exclusive, but I never agreed to sit around and talk about him."

"I don't want to talk about him," he growled. "I just want to get to know you. I want to understand why you feel I'm not a good match for you."

"God, don't you see it?" she sighed. "I want, I want. You said so yourself, you always get what you want. And that's why I feel the way I do. I've dated too many guys who *want*. But none of them want to give. They're too concerned with getting *their* way, advancing *their* careers, and I always come in second. Well, I'm sick of it. Doug may not be the most exciting man on the planet, but he wants the same things I do—a solid marriage, a stable home, and *that's* what I want out of a relationship."

A deafening silence fell over the room, stretching between. Brody felt like throwing something. He resented the fact that Hayden was projecting her frustration with her father and the previous men in her life onto him, but, hell, he'd opened this can of worms. Pushed her too far, too fast. Needled her about her on-hold relationship and demanded she give him a chance she wasn't ready to give.

Would he still get that chance now? Or had he blown it completely?

"I think asking you over here was a bad idea," she said.

The answer to his silent question became painfully clear.

He'd blown it, all right.

Big-time.

THE LAST THING Hayden felt like doing on Sunday night was attending a birthday party for a wealthy entrepreneur she didn't even know, but when she'd called her father to try to get out of it, he wouldn't have it. He'd insisted her presence was essential, though she honestly didn't know why. Every time she socialized with her father and his friends she ended up standing at the bar by herself.

But she didn't want to let down her dad. And considering how she'd left things with Brody on Friday night, maybe it was better to get out of that big penthouse and away from her thoughts.

It was just past eight o'clock when she neared the Gallagher Club, a prestigious men's club in one of Chicago's most historical neighborhoods. It had been founded by Walter Gallagher, a filthy rich entrepreneur who'd decided he needed to build a place where other filthy rich entrepreneurs could congregate.

The Gallagher Club was by invitation only, and it took some men decades to gain membership. Her father had inherited the membership when he'd purchased the Warriors from their previous owner, and he loved flaunting it. When Hayden was in town, he never took her anywhere else.

She drove down the wide, tree-lined street, slowing her rented Honda Civic when she spotted a crowd at the end of the road. As she got closer, she noticed a few news vans. The dozen or so people milling by the curb were reporters.

And since she couldn't think of anyone else currently involved in a possible criminal investigation, she knew the press was there because of her father.

This was not good.

Taking a few calming breaths, she drove through the wrought-iron gates leading to the Gallagher Club, turning her head and averting her eyes when a few of the reporters started to peer in at her. She exhaled as she steered up the circular cobblestone driveway and slowed the car behind the line of vehicles waiting near the valet area.

Had the reporters harassed her father when he'd driven in? Had he stopped to speak with them, to deny the absurd news report?

A voice interrupted the troubling thoughts. "Good evening, madam."

She lifted her head and saw a young man in a burgundy valet uniform hovering over the driver's window.

"May I take your keys?" he asked.

Her gaze flitted to the massive mansion with its enormous limestone pillars and the stone statues lining the marble entrance. Her father was probably already in there, most likely smoking cigars with his rich friends and acting as if the presence of the media didn't bother him. But she knew it had to bug him. Presley's reputation mattered to him more than anything.

With another sigh, she handed the valet her keys and stepped out of the car. "Davis will escort you inside," the young man informed her.

Davis turned out to be a tall, bulky man in a black tuxedo who extended his arm and led her up the front steps toward the two oak doors at the entrance.

He opened one door and said, "Enjoy your evening."

"Thank you," she answered, then stepped into the lavish foyer.

Miles of black marble spanned the front hall, and overhead a sparkling crystal chandelier dangled from the high ceiling. When she took a breath, she inhaled the scent of wine, cologne and all things expensive.

She paused next to the entrance of the coat check and quickly glanced down to make sure there were no wardrobe mishaps happening. She'd worn a slinky silver dress that clung to her curves, emphasizing her cleavage and bottom. Not to mention that it was slit up to the thigh, revealing a lot of leg. A light touch of eye makeup and some shiny pink lip gloss, and the ensemble had been complete.

Annoyingly, she'd thought about Brody the entire time she'd gotten ready. How much he'd probably enjoy seeing her in the dress—and how much he'd love taking it off her.

It still bothered her, how they'd left things Friday night. Brody hadn't spent the night, needing to catch his flight in the morning, and he'd headed for the elevator with the air of a man leaving a battlefield in defeat.

She'd felt pretty defeated, too. What had she been thinking, suggesting they go out on a real date? After all, she was the one who'd made it clear she wanted a fling. Yet she'd really enjoyed their conversation—talking to him about art, hearing about his parents. It had been really nice. Comfortable. And before she knew it, she was falling right back into her old ways, looking to embark on a new relationship.

That Brody had to be in L.A. the next day was just the wake-up call she'd needed. It reminded her precisely what she wanted—someone stable. Someone who wouldn't be out of town for half the year, while their relationship took second place. As wildly attracted to Brody as she was, she knew he couldn't be that someone.

"Quade has outdone himself this year," a male voice boomed, interrupting her thoughts and reminding her where she was.

Smoothing out the front of her dress, she followed the group of tuxedo-clad men into the large ballroom off to the left. It was a black-tie event, and she found herself surrounded by beautifully dressed people, some older, some younger, all strangers. A dance floor graced the center of the room, in front of a live band that was belting out an upbeat swing song. Before she could blink, a waiter handed her a glass of champagne.

Just as she was about to take a sip, a familiar face caught her eye.

"Darcy?" she called in surprise.

Her best friend's silky red hair swung over her shoulders as she spun around. "Hey! What are you doing here?"

"My dad demanded I make an appearance." She grimaced. "And to think, I almost believed he wanted to spend some time with me."

Bitter much?

Fine, so she was bitter, but really, who could blame her? She'd come here to support her father and bridge the distance between them, and yet he seemed determined to avoid spending quality time with her.

"What are *you* doing here?" she asked Darcy.

Her friend was clad in a white minidress that contrasted nicely with her bright red hair and vibrant blue eyes. "I know the birthday boy. He's a regular at the boutique and pretty much threatened to take his business elsewhere if I didn't make an appearance." Darcy snorted. "To be honest, I think he's dying to get into my panties. Like *that* will ever happen."

"Who exactly is the birthday boy? Dad neglected to mention."

"Jonas Quade," Darcy answered. "He's filthy rich, calls himself a philanthropist, and spends thousands of dollars on his many mistresses. Oh, and he's also a pompous ass, but I can't complain because those thousands I mentioned, well, he spends them at my boutique. He likes getting his lady friends to try on lace teddies and model for him, that sleazy bastar— Crap, here he comes."

A gray-haired man with the build of Arnold Schwarzenegger and a George Hamilton tan made a beeline in their direction. A plump, blond woman tagged on his heels, looking annoyed by her escort's obvious enthusiasm for Darcy.

"Darcy!" Jonas Quade boomed, grinning widely. "What a treat to see you here."

"Happy birthday, Mr. Quade," Darcy said politely.

Quade turned to his companion. "Margaret, this is the owner of the lingerie store where I buy you all those *intimate* gifts." He winked at the blonde. "Darcy, this is my wife, Margaret."

Hayden could see the barely contained mirth on her friend's face. Hayden had to wonder if Quade's wife was aware that her husband wasn't buying intimate gifts only for her.

"And who is your lovely friend?" Quade asked, peering at Hayden.

Since she didn't particularly enjoy being ogled, Hayden felt a flicker of relief when, before Darcy could introduce them, Quade's wife suddenly latched on to his arm and said, "Marcus is trying to get your attention, darling." She proceeded to forcibly drag him away from the two women.

"Enjoy the party," Quade called over his shoulder.

"That poor woman," Darcy said. "She has no idea…"

"I'm sure she knows. He might as well have *adulterer* tattooed on his forehead."

She and Darcy started to giggle, and Hayden decided this party might not be so bad after all. She hadn't spotted her father yet, but with Darcy by her side, she might not have such an awful time.

"Can I interest you in a dance?"

Damn, she should've known her best friend, with that indecently short dress, wouldn't be available for long.

The handsome, dark-haired man in a navy-blue pinstriped suit eyed Darcy expectantly. After a moment she shrugged, and said, "I'd love to dance." She handed her champagne flute to Hayden, adding, "I'll catch up with you later, okay?"

"Sure. Have fun."

Hayden's shoulders sagged as her friend followed Handsome Man onto the dance floor. Great. Seeing Darcy had been a pleasant surprise, but now her enthusiasm returned to its original level: low.

Then it swiftly dropped to nonexistent.

"Hayden, honey!" Her father's commanding voice sliced through the loud chatter and strains of music. He strode up to her, a glass of bourbon in his hand and an unlit cigar poking out of the corner of his mouth.

She stood on her tiptoes and pecked his cheek. "Hey, Dad. You look like you're enjoying yourself."

"I am, I am." He squeezed her arm and beamed at her. "You look gorgeous."

Something about his overly broad smile troubled her. She wasn't sure why—he was just smiling. And yet an alarm went off in her head. She examined her father more closely. His face was flushed and his eyes were a touch too bright.

Like an unwanted visit from the Avon lady, Sheila's words filled her head. *Your father's drinking again.*

"Are you okay?" she asked, unable to stop the wariness from seeping into her tone. "You look a little…tense."

He waved a hand dismissively. "I'm absolutely great."

"You sure? Because I saw those reporters outside and…" And what? *And I wanted to make sure that they're all just lying about your involvement in illegal sports betting?*

Presley's eyes darkened. "Ignore those bloodsuckers. They're only trying to cause trouble, conjuring up their delusional stories to sell papers." He took a slug of bourbon. "This isn't the time to discuss this. Martin Hargrove was just asking me about you. You remember Martin, he owns a chain of restaurants—"

"Dad, you can't just ignore this," she cut in. "What about the announcement that one of your players came forward? I tried calling your cell yesterday afternoon to talk about it but I kept getting your voice mail. I left you two messages."

He ignored the last statement and said, "I was golfing with Judge Harrison. No cell service out on the course."

She decided not to mention that she'd also called the house he was renting, knowing he'd probably have an excuse for not answering those calls, too.

God, why was he acting like none of this was a big deal? One of his players had admitted that Presley fixed games, and her father was brushing it off like a fleck of lint on his sleeve. Going to parties, smoking cigars, mingling with friends. Did he honestly think this would all just blow over? Hayden refused to believe her father had done the things he was accused of, but she wasn't naive enough to think they could just close their eyes and blink the whole mess away.

"Did you at least talk to Judge Harrison about what your next move should be?" she asked.

"Why the hell would I do that?"

"Because this is starting to get serious." Hayden clenched her fists at her sides. "You should give a press conference maintaining your innocence. Or at the very least, talk to your lawyer."

He didn't bother replying, just shrugged, then lifted his drink to his mouth. After swallowing the rest of the liquid, he signaled a passing waiter and swiped a glass of champagne.

Hayden took the opportunity to place her and Darcy's drinks on the waiter's tray, suddenly losing any taste for alcohol. Both times she'd seen her father this past week, he'd been drinking, but tonight it was obvious her father was drunk. His rosy cheeks and glazed eyes, the way he was swaying on his feet. The blatant case of denial.

"Dad…how much have you had to drink?"

His features instantly hardened. "Pardon me?"

"You just seem a little…buzzed," she said for lack of a better word.

"Buzzed? Is that California slang for drunk?" He frowned. "I can assure you, Hayden, I am not drunk. I've only had a couple drinks."

The defensive note in his voice deepened her concern. When people started making excuses for their inebriated state…wasn't that a sign of a drinking problem?

She cursed her stepmother for putting all these absurd ideas into her head. Her father wasn't an alcoholic. He didn't have a drinking problem, he hadn't had an affair, and he certainly hadn't illegally fixed any Warrior games to make a profit.

Right?

Her temples began to throb. God, she didn't want to doubt her dad, the man who'd raised her alone, the man who up until a few years ago had been her closest friend.

She opened her mouth to apologize, but he cut her off before she could. "I'm sick of these accusations, you hear me?"

She blinked. "What? Dad—"

"I get enough flak from Sheila, I don't need to hear this shit from my own daughter."

His eyes were on fire, his cheeks crimson with anger, and she found herself taking a step back. Tears stung her eyes. Oh, God. For the first time in her life she was frightened of her own father.

"So I made a few bad investments. Sue me," he growled, his champagne glass shaking along with his hands. "It doesn't make me a criminal. Don't you dare accuse me of that."

She swallowed. "I wasn't—"

"I didn't fix those games," he snapped. "And I don't have a drinking problem."

A ragged breath escaped his lips, the stale odor of alcohol burning her nostrils and betraying his last statement. Her father *was* drunk. This time there wasn't a single doubt in her mind. As she stood there, stunned, a tear crept down her cheek.

"Hayden…honey…oh, Lord, I'm sorry. I didn't mean to snap at you like that."

She didn't answer, just swallowed again and swiped at her face with a shaky hand.

Her father reached out and touched her shoulder. "Forgive me."

Before she could respond, Jonas Quade approached with jovial strides, clasped his hand on Presley's arm and said, "There you are, Pres. My son Gregory is dying to meet you. He's the Warriors' number-one fan."

Her father's dark green eyes pleaded with her, relaying the message he couldn't voice at the moment. *We'll talk about this later.*

She managed a nod, then drew in a ragged breath as Quade led her father away.

The second the two men ambled off, she spun on her heel and hurried to the French doors leading to the patio, hoping she could keep any more tears at bay until she was out of sight.

8

"I REALLY WISH you hadn't dragged me here," Sam Becker groaned as he drove his shiny silver Lexus in the direction of the Gallagher Club. "My wife is pissed."

"Come on, Mary doesn't have a 'pissed' bone in her body," Brody replied, thinking of the tiny, delicate woman who'd been married to Sam for fifteen years.

"That's what she wants you to think. Trust me, behind closed doors she's not very nice."

Brody laughed.

"I swear, she almost tore my head off when I told her I was going out with you tonight. It was last-minute, so we couldn't get a babysitter for Tamara. Mary had to cancel her plans. I'll never hear the end of this. Thanks a lot, kiddo."

Sam's words might have evoked guilt in some men, but Brody couldn't muster any. For two days he'd been trying to come up with a way to see Hayden and make things right. Sure, he could've just called her, but the way things had ended at the penthouse the other night left him cautious.

Hayden had mentioned she'd be at the Gallagher Club tonight, and he'd spent the entire afternoon wondering how he could show up there without appearing desperate. The answer had come to him during a call from Becker, who'd phoned to discuss a charity event they were participating in next month.

Brody wasn't a member of the Gallagher Club, but Becker was, so Brody had promptly ordered his best bud to brush the dust off his tuxedo.

He felt bad that Becker had been raked over the coals by his wife, but he'd make it up to him.

"Why didn't you get Lucy to watch Tamara?" Brody asked. He'd been over to Becker's house dozens of times, and had spent quite a bit of time with Becker's two daughters. Lucy was fourteen, ten years older than her sister Tamara, but it had been obvious to Brody how much the teenager loved her baby sister.

"Lucy has a—God help me—" Becker groaned "—boyfriend. They're at the movies tonight."

Brody hooted. "You actually let her leave the house with the guy?"

"I had no choice. Mary said I couldn't threaten him with a shotgun." Becker sighed. "And speaking of shotguns, she told me to put one to your head if you didn't agree to spend a week at our lake house this summer. She renovated the entire place and is dying to show it off."

Brody usually tried to spend the entire summer in Michigan with his parents, but for Becker, he was willing to alter his plans. "Tell your wife I'll be there. Just name the date."

Becker suddenly slowed the car. "Oh, shit."

A small crowd of reporters hovered in front of the gates of the Gallagher Club. A few turned their heads at the Lexus's approach.

Rolling up the windows, Becker turned to Brody and said, "Obviously the vultures are following dear old Pres."

Brody suppressed a groan. "Are you surprised? Someone on the team came forward and confirmed the rumors. The press is salivating."

Becker drove through the gate and stopped in front of the waiting valet. Lips tight, he got out of the car without a word.

The second Brody's feet connected with the cobblestone driveway, one of the reporters shouted at them from the gate.

"Becker! Croft!" a man yelled, practically poking his entire bald head between two of the gate's bars. "Any comment on the allegations that Presley Houston fixed Warriors games and…"

Brody tuned the guy out, choosing instead to follow Becker up the front steps toward the entrance of the club.

"Jeez, I hate this place," Becker muttered as they entered the foyer.

"How'd you get to be a member anyway?" Brody asked the question without caring too much about the answer. He'd much rather talk to Becker about Craig Wyatt and the possibility that he was the one who'd come forward, but Becker's body language clearly said he didn't want to discuss the reporters or the scandal. His massive shoulders were tight, his square jaw clenched. Brody could understand. He'd been feeling tense himself ever since he'd watched that news story with Hayden.

And yesterday's loss in Los Angeles hadn't helped. Losing a play-off game was bad, but losing 6–0 was pathetic. The Warriors had played like a team of amateurs, and though nobody had spoken about the scandal, Brody knew it was on their minds. He'd found himself glancing around the locker room, wondering which one of the guys had confessed to knowing about the bribes.

"My wife is involved with one of Jonas Quade's charity foundations," Becker was saying in response Brody's question. "When he offered to put in a good word for me with the members' committee, Mary pretty much threatened divorce unless I joined." Becker muttered a curse. "I'm telling you, man, she's not a nice person."

"You must have seen *something* good in her considering you married the woman."

"Yeah, I did see something." Becker's rugged features softened. "My soul mate."

The two men entered the massive ballroom, and Brody's eyes instantly began darting around the room.

"So what's her name?" Becker asked with a sigh.

He blinked. "What?"

"Come on, Croft. Only reason you dragged me here is because I belong to this pretentious society of snobs and you needed to score an invite. And since you're no social climber, that means you came here to see a woman. So what's her name?"

"Hayden," he admitted.

Becker accepted a glass of wine from a passing waiter. "Is she a member of Chicago's high society?"

"Kind of." He hesitated. "She's Presley's daughter."

Becker paused mid-sip. "As in the daughter of Presley Houston, the man who signs our paychecks?"

"Yep."

"Bad idea, man. You don't want to get involved with a Houston, not while this betting bullshit is going on."

Brody's tuxedo jacket suddenly felt too tight. "Hayden has nothing to do with that. She's just visiting from California."

"And if the media finds out you're sleeping with her, they'll start drooling. It'll be all over the headlines, how Pres's daughter is screwing one of the star players on the team in order to shut him up."

The hairs on the back of Brody's neck stood on end. "You say that as if you think there's something I need shutting up about. Sam…do you know something about this bribery crap?"

"No, of course not."

"You sure?" He hesitated. "You didn't…you didn't take a bribe, did you?"

Becker looked as if he'd been shot by a bazooka. His mouth dropped open, his cheeks reddened and a vein popped out in his forehead. "You actually think I'd take a fucking bribe? I've been playing in this league for half my life. Trust me, I earn enough."

Brody relaxed. "I didn't think you took a bribe," he said, trying to inject reassurance into his voice. "But what you just said…it sounds like you know more about this scandal than the rest of us. Did Pres tell you anything?"

Though he looked calm now, the vein on Becker's forehead continued to throb. He seemed uncomfortable, scanning the room like that of a prisoner scouting out an escape route. "I don't know anything," he finally said.

"Well, I think I might," Brody found himself confessing.

Becker's head jerked up. "What are you talking about?"

Although this was probably not the time, and definitely not the place, Brody told Becker about what he'd seen at the arena the other day. He spoke in a hushed tone, revealing his suspicions that Sheila Houston had confided in Craig Wyatt about whatever it was she knew, and that Wyatt was the one who'd spoken to the league. He finished with, "So do you think I should do something?"

The other man released a ragged breath. He looked a bit shell-shocked. "Honestly? I think it would be a bad idea."

"Why do you say that?"

"You don't want to get involved," Becker warned in a low voice. "You'll only cast suspicion on yourself."

He mulled over his friend's advice, knowing Becker did have a point. But then he thought of the team captain, and how subdued Wyatt had been lately. Wyatt had always been serious, but he'd barely spoken a word to anyone in weeks, and when he did, it was to yell at them for making a mistake out on the ice. Brody got the feeling Craig Wyatt might very well be in need of a friend, and as reluctant as he was to get involved, he wasn't sure he could watch a teammate struggle without doing a thing to help.

But Becker remained firm. "Don't confront Craig, kiddo. If it bothers you this much, I'll talk to him, okay?"

He glanced at his friend in surprise. "You'd really do that?"

With a playful punch to Brody's arm, Becker gave a faint smile and said, "Unlike my old-timer self, you've still got a lot of years ahead of you. I don't want to see your career tank just because Presley Houston might've decided he needed some extra cash."

"My two favorite players!"

Speak of the devil. Brody shot Becker a look of gratitude, then pasted on a smile as Presley approached them, holding a glass of champagne in his large hand. Considering there were reporters outside just dying to roast Pres for these bribery charges, the man seemed surprisingly jovial. Either the allegations didn't concern him, or he was doing a damn good job covering up his distress.

"Having a good time?" Pres asked.

"We just got here," answered Becker.

"Well, the party's just getting started." Pres lifted his glass to his lips and emptied it. A second later he flagged down a waiter and promptly received a full glass.

"Is your daughter here tonight?" Brody asked. His voice came out more eager than casual. His peripheral vision caught Becker's mouth creasing in a frown.

Pres looked distinctly ill at ease at the mention of Hayden. "I think she went out on the patio," he said.

And there was his cue.

Brody didn't feel bad leaving Becker in the clutches of the obviously plastered team owner. Sam Becker had been in the business long enough to know how to handle every situation thrown at him, and he usually handled them as well as he did the puck. The man was a pro, through and through.

Brody stepped away, glancing around the enormous ballroom for the patio entrance. Finally he spotted the French doors and made his way toward them.

His breath caught at the sight of Hayden's silver-clad figure. She was leaning against the railing overlooking the grounds of the estate, her long brown hair cascading down her bare shoulders, her delectable ass hugged by the silky material of her dress.

He paused at the doors, admiring her. To his surprise, she turned abruptly as if sensing his presence. Their eyes locked. And that's when he saw that her sooty black lashes were spiky with tears.

He was by her side in seconds. "Hey, what's wrong?" he murmured, resting both hands on her slender waist and pulling her toward him.

She sank into his embrace and pressed her face against his shoulder as she whispered, "What are you doing here?"

"I tagged along with a friend." He gently stroked her back. "And I'm glad I did. You look awful."

"Gee, thanks." Her voice came out muffled against the front of his tuxedo jacket.

"Oh, quit sulking. You know you're the sexiest woman at this party." He swept a hand over her firm bottom. The feel of her warm, curvy body made his pulse quicken, but he reminded himself that now was not the time.

"Now tell me the reason for *these*." He brushed the moisture from her lashes. "What happened?"

"Nothing."

"Hayden."

She lifted her head, chin tilting with defiance. "It's not a big deal, Brody. Just go inside and enjoy the party."

"Screw the party. I came here to see you."

"Well, I came here to see my dad." She turned her head away and stared out at the landscaped grounds.

The temperature had dipped drastically and the thick gray clouds littering the night sky hinted at a storm. Already the endless carpet of flowers on the lush lawn was starting to sway in the wind, sweeping a sweet aroma in the direction of the cobblestone patio.

It was the kind of night he usually enjoyed, the moistness of the air, the hint of rain and thunder, but he couldn't appreciate it when Hayden looked so distraught.

And beautiful. Damn, but she also looked beautiful. The slinky silver dress, the strappy heels, the shiny pink gloss coating her sensual lips. He wanted her, as strongly and as violently as he'd wanted her that first night in the bar. And not just sexually. Something about this woman brought out a protective, nurturing side in him he'd never known he possessed.

"Please, Hayden, tell me what happened."

She hesitated for so long he didn't think she'd say anything, but then her mouth opened and a string of words flew out like bullets spitting from a rifle.

"I think my father is drinking. He blew up at me when I questioned him about it, and then he made a few remarks about bad investments." She looked up, her eyes wide with anguish. "I'm worried he might have done some of the things everyone is accusing him of. God, Brody, I think there's actually a chance he might have bribed players and bet on games."

Brody's heart plummeted to the pit of his stomach. He shoved his fists into the pockets of his jacket, hoping to bring warmth to hands that had suddenly grown ice-cold. Damn it. He didn't want to have this conversation, especially with Hayden. Not when his own flags were raised.

So he just stood there in silence, waiting for her to continue and hoping she wouldn't ask him any questions that might force him to reveal something she probably wouldn't want to hear.

"I don't know what I should do," she murmured. "I don't

know how to help him. I don't know if he's guilty or innocent. I have no proof he has a drinking problem, but it's obvious after tonight that something is going on with my dad."

"You need to try talking to him when he's sober," Brody advised.

"I've tried," she moaned with frustration. "But he's determined not to be alone with me. And if by chance we *are* alone, he changes the subject every time I try to bring up my concerns. He won't let me in, Brody."

They stood there for a moment, silently, his arms wrapped around her slender body, her head tucked against his chest.

"I never thought my relationship with my dad would get to this point," she whispered. "He treated me like a stranger tonight. He snapped at me, *cursed* at me, looked right through me, as if I was just another headache he didn't want to deal with instead of his only daughter."

Brody threaded his fingers through her hair and stroked the soft tresses while he caressed her cheek with his other hand. "Did you two used to be close?" he asked.

"Very." She gave a soft sigh. "Nowadays, the team comes first."

"I'm sure that's not true."

She raised her chin and met his eyes. "Tell me, in all the years you've played for the Warriors, how many times has my father mentioned me?"

Discomfort coiled in his gut. "A bunch of times," he said vaguely.

Her eyes pierced his. "Really?"

"Fine, never," he admitted. "But I'm just a player to your father. He's certainly never treated me as a confidant."

"My dad is obsessed with the team," she said flatly. "He's always loved hockey, but when he was just a coach, it wasn't this bad. Now that he owns a team, he's almost fanatical. It used to be about the game for him. Somehow it's become about making money, being as powerful as he can be."

"Money and power aren't bad things to want," Brody had to point out.

"Sure, but what about family? Who are you supposed to rely on when the money and power are gone? Who will be there to love you?"

A cloud of sadness floated across her pretty face, her expression growing bittersweet. "You know he used to take me fishing a lot? Every summer we'd rent a cabin up at the lake, usually for an entire week. We moved around so much, but Dad always managed to find a place to go fishing. I hated to fish, but I pretended to love it because I wanted to spend the time with my dad."

She moved out of his arms and walked back to the railing, leaning forward and breathing in the cool night air. Without turning around, she continued speaking. "We stopped going once I moved to California. He always promised we'd go back to the lake during my visits home, but we never got around to it. Though we did go out on the yacht last summer." She made a face. "Sheila spent the entire trip talking about her nails. And Dad was on the phone the whole time."

The wistful note in her voice struck a chord of sympathy in him. Despite his busy schedule, he always made sure to return to Michigan a few times a year to see his parents. In the off-season he stayed with them for a month and spent every available moment with his folks. Although it irked him a little that his mom refused to quit her hairdressing job and take advantage of her son's wealth, he loved being home with his folks. And they were always thrilled to have him. He couldn't imagine his parents ever being too busy to hang out with their only son.

Presley Houston was an idiot. There was no other explanation for why the man would pass up the opportunity to spend time with a daughter as incredible as Hayden. She was intelligent, warm, passionate.

"I don't want to talk about this anymore," she burst out. "There's no point. Dad and I have been drifting apart for years. I was stupid to think he might actually value my support."

"I'm sure he does value it. It's obvious he's been drinking tonight, babe. It was probably the alcohol that made him snap at you like that."

"Alcohol is no excuse." She raked her fingers through her hair and scowled. "God, I need to get out of here. I want to go someplace where I can hear my own thoughts."

He glanced at the watch he'd picked up from the arena earlier in the morning, saw it wasn't that late, and threw an arm around Hayden's shoulders. "I know just the place."

She studied him warily, as if she suddenly remembered what had transpired between them two nights ago. He saw her hesitation, her reluctance to let him back in, but thankfully she made no protest when he took her hand. Instead, she clasped her warm fingers in his and said, "Let's go."

"THIS IS IT? The place where all my thoughts will become clear?" Hayden couldn't help but laugh as she followed Brody into the dark hockey arena twenty minutes later.

She'd let Brody drive her car, but hadn't thought to ask where he was taking her. She'd been content to sit in silence, trying to make sense of everything her father had said to her tonight. Now she kind of wished she'd been more curious about their destination.

The night guard had let them in. He'd seemed surprised at the sight of Brody Croft showing up at the practice arena way after hours, but didn't object to Brody's request. After digging up an old pair of boys' skates for Hayden from the equipment room, the guard had unlocked the doors leading out to the rink, flicked on the lights and disappeared with a smile.

"Trust me," Brody said. "There's nothing like the feel of ice under your skates to clear your head."

"Uh, I should probably mention I haven't ice-skated since I was a kid."

He looked aghast. "But your father owns a hockey team."

"We're not allowed to talk about my father anymore tonight, remember?"

"Right. Sorry." He flashed a charming grin. "Don't worry, I'll make sure you don't fall flat on your ass. Now sit."

Obligingly, she sat on the hard wooden bench and allowed Brody to remove her high heels. He caressed her stockinged feet for a moment, then reached for the skates the guard had found and helped her get a foot into one.

"It's tight," she complained.

"It belongs to a twelve-year-old boy. No figure skates here, so you'll have to make do."

Brody laced up the skates for her, then flopped down on the bench and kicked off his shiny black dress shoes. He'd retrieved a spare pair of skates from the bottom of his locker, and he put them on expertly, grinning when he saw her wobble to her feet. She made quite a fashion statement in her party dress and scuffed black hockey skates.

She held out her arms in an attempt to balance herself. "I'm totally going to fall on my butt," she said.

"I told you, I won't let it happen."

He stood, took two steps forward and unlatched the wooden gate that ringed the ice. Like the pro hockey player he was, he slid onto the rink effortlessly and skated backward for a moment while she stood at the gate and muttered, "Show-off."

Laughing, he moved toward her and held out his hand.

She stared at his long, calloused fingers, wanting so badly to grab onto them and never let go. Yet another part of her was hesitant. When she'd picked him up at the bar five days ago, she hadn't imagined she'd see him after that first night. Or that she'd sleep with him again. Or that she might actually start to *like* him.

And she did like him. As much as she wanted to continue viewing Brody as nothing more than a one-night stand who'd rocked her world, he was becoming unnervingly real to her. He'd listened when she'd babbled about art, he'd let her cry on his shoulder, he'd brought her to this dark arena just to take her mind off her worries. One-night stands weren't supposed to do that, darn it!

"Come on, Hayden, I won't let you fall," he reassured her.

With a nod of acceptance, she took his hand. The second the blades of her skates connected with the sleek ice, she almost keeled over. Her arms windmilled, her legs spread open, and her skates moved in opposite directions as if trying to force her into the splits.

Brody promptly steadied her. "You're not very good at this, are you?"

"I told you I wasn't," she returned with an indignant glare. "Ask me to lecture you about Impressionist art, I can do that. But skating? I suck."

"Because you're trying to walk instead of glide," he pointed out. He clamped both his hands on her waist. "Quit doing that. Now, take my hand and do what I'm doing."

Slowly, they pushed forward again. While Brody's strides were effortless, hers were clumsy. Every few feet the tips of her skates would dig into the ice and she'd lurch forward, but Brody stayed true to his word. He didn't let her fall. Not even once.

"There you go," he exclaimed. "You're getting the hang of it."

She couldn't help smiling. Once she'd taken his advice and stopped treating the skates as shoes, her movements had become smoother. She felt giddy as they picked up speed, gliding along the ice like a pair of Thoroughbreds rounding a racetrack.

The boards, the benches, the bleachers—it all whizzed by her, the cool air in the arena reddening her cheeks. Although there were goose bumps dotting her bare arms, she didn't mind the cold temperature. The chill in the arena soothed her, cleansing her mind.

She cast a sideways glance at Brody and saw he was enjoying this, too. God, he looked delicious in his tuxedo. The jacket stretched over his broad shoulders and powerful chest, and the slightly loose trousers didn't hide his taut behind. She noticed his bow tie sat a little crooked, and resisted the urge to reach out and straighten it. She didn't want to move her arms and risk falling, so she tightened her fingers around his instead.

He looked down at their intertwined fingers, his mouth parting slightly, as if he wanted to speak but was being cautious. She knew exactly what was on his mind, because the same thing was running through hers. God help her, but she wanted this man in her bed again.

He was arrogant, yes, and pushy sometimes. But he also turned her on in the fiercest way, and every time he fixed those midnight-blue eyes on her, every time he wrapped those big arms around her, she melted.

They slowed their pace, and she forced her thoughts away from the dangerous territory they'd crossed into and tried to come up with a neutral topic of conversation. One that didn't make her think of Brody, naked and hard as he devoured her body with his tongue.

"When did you start playing?" she finally asked, deciding his career was as safe a subject as any.

"Pretty much the second I could walk, I was learning to skate. My dad used to take me to this outdoor rink near our house in Michigan." He chuckled. "Well, it wasn't much of a rink. Just a crappy pond that froze over every winter. My parents couldn't afford the membership fee for a real arena, so I used to practice my slap shots out on that pond while my dad sat on a folding chair in the snow and read car magazines."

"Did you play on a school team?"

"Uh, what team *wasn't* I on?" He dropped her hand and began skating lazy circles around her. "In high school I played hockey, rugby and baseball in the spring. Oh, and I was on the lacrosse team until the practices started to interfere with my hockey schedule."

"Huh. So you were one of *those* guys. I bet you were voted Most Likely to Become a Pro Athlete in your high school yearbook."

"Actually, I was."

He told her a bit about his early years in the league, then made her laugh with some anecdotes about his parents and their overwhelming pride in him. At times a twinge of bitterness seeped into his voice, giving her the feeling that his childhood was tougher than he let on, but she didn't pry. She remembered him telling her money had been tight for his family, and it was obviously something he didn't like talking about.

A few minutes later, a cramp seized her leg and she wobbled to a stop, leaning against the splintered sideboards as she rubbed the back of her thigh. On the West Coast she jogged every morning before heading over to the university, but she was obviously not in the great shape she'd believed herself to be in. Her legs were aching and they'd only been skating around for twenty minutes.

"Wanna take a break?" Brody offered.

"Please."

They stepped off the ice and climbed up to the bleachers. Brody was an expert when it came to walking on skates. She wasn't so fortunate. She almost pitched forward a half-dozen times before she finally sank down on the bench and exhaled with relief.

"I think I pulled a muscle in my butt," she grumbled.

"Want me to rub the kinks out?"

She stiffened, wishing his voice didn't contain that husky note of erotic promise. Damn it. She couldn't fall into bed with him again. As thrilling as it would be to continue exploring the sexual canvas they seemed so skilled at painting together, she couldn't help remembering what had happened the last time she'd given in.

As if sensing her concerns, Brody let out an unsteady breath. "I'm sorry about the other night, Hayden. I acted like an ass."

She didn't reply, just offered a pointed nod.

"I know I'm rough around the edges. I'm demanding, I like getting my way and I'm definitely not the kind of man who's content with playing second fiddle." He held up his hand before she could cut in. "I shouldn't have hassled you about, you know, *Doug*—" he said the name like it was contagious "—but damn it, Hayden, it drives me crazy knowing there's someone else in your life. I'm not used to sharing."

"You're not sharing. Doug and I are on a break."

"There's a giant difference between a break and a breakup." He frowned. "Do you think you'll go back to him?"

"I don't know." Deep down, though, she knew the answer to that question and it probably wasn't one Doug was going to like. But she couldn't talk about it, not now, and definitely not with Brody.

She could tell he wasn't happy with her answer, but instead of challenging her the way he had two nights ago, he simply nodded. "Guess I'll have to live it with then. And I *can* live with it, especially if it means I get to spend more time with you."

"But why? What do you see in me that makes you so sure we should pursue this?" She wasn't prone to insecurities, but she couldn't quite figure out why this sexy giant of a man wanted *her* and not some supermodel.

"What do I see in you?" He leaned closer. "You want a list? I can do that. I'll skip how beautiful you are. That's all just superficial."

"I'm not above superficial."

He chuckled. "So you'd like me to start with your wild green eyes that have been knocking me out since the second you strolled up to that pool table?"

She bit her lower lip. "Okay."

Carefully, he took a lock of her hair between his fingers. "Or should I start with this silky brown hair that keeps making me want to reach out and touch it?" His attention dropped to her chest. "Or these breasts I can't get enough of?" The fingers that had been toying with her hair moved to brush over her nipples, which were pushing against the thin fabric of her dress. "Or maybe these lips that keep begging me to taste them?" He brushed a thumb over her bottom lip.

Her lips parted, her eyelids grew heavy, and thankfully she was sitting down because she didn't think she could hold up the weight of her body in her weakened state. This man was one smooth talker.

"Any of those places are fine," she breathed.

Strong hands cupped her face. "Then there's the intelligence that practically radiates from you. Did I ever tell you smart women seriously turn me on?" His thumbs began caressing her cheeks and he bent to whisper close to her ear. "You're a walking contradiction, Hayden. Prim and proper one moment, wild and uninhibited the next. And the more I get to know you, the more I like what I find."

Each of his words softened her heart, and every warm wisp of his breath against her ear made her quiver with need.

"When I left the penthouse the other night you wouldn't let me kiss you," he said, his lips just inches from hers. "I promised myself I wouldn't kiss you again until you asked me to."

"Kiss me, Brody. Please…"

In an instant, his lips touched hers, unleashing a trickle of soothing warmth that rivaled a shot of fine brandy. She moved a hand to his cheek and relished the light prickles of his five-o'clock shadow. And despite his tender touch, the hardness of his chest and the roughness of his cheek reminded her he was all man.

He groaned softly, and deepened the kiss. She parted her lips, inviting him to explore. She wanted to surround herself in his protective embrace. Her father's behavior tonight had frightened her, hurt her, but Brody's kiss made her forget about everything except this moment, the feel of his mouth on hers, the flick of his tongue and warm caress of his fingers on her cheek.

She slid her hand to the nape of his neck, allowing the soft curls to tickle her fingers. She took hold and pulled the kiss deeper. His slow, heavy groan spoke of acceptance and thanks.

His hands moved down her sides, and he lightly caressed the sides of her breasts with his thumbs, sending a pulsing charge through her system. It was the most gentle he'd ever been with her, a stark change from his rough, drugging kisses and eager exploratory hands. And as much as she was enjoying the kiss, she wanted more. She lowered her hands to the growing bulge in his tuxedo trousers, but he moved her hand away and broke the kiss.

For a moment, her eyes wouldn't open and her mouth

wouldn't close. She was held in transition, her body still tingling from his touch. As she slowly raised her lids, she saw the deep sense of need in his eyes. Need that matched hers.

"Close your eyes," he murmured.

"Why?"

"Just do it."

Curious, she let her eyelids flutter shut. She heard a rustling sound, felt Brody move closer and lean forward, then gasped when his hand circled her ankle.

"Don't move." His voice was barely above a whisper.

She swallowed. Waiting. Sighing when he ran his big warm hand up her leg, bunching her dress between his fingers as he traveled north. His touch suffused her with heat, made her pulse race. He glided his fingers along her inner thigh, leaving a trail of fire in his wake. And then his palm was pressed against her lace panties.

"What are you doing?" she breathed out.

"De-stressing you." His tongue was suddenly on her ear, flicking against the tender lobe before suckling it.

Silent laughter shook her as her eyes popped open. "What's with you and your need to intimately touch me in public?"

He rubbed his palm against her mound, his breath hot against her ear as he whispered, "Want me to stop?"

"God, no."

"Good."

He moved his hand under her panties and pushed one long finger deep into her hot channel.

"You're always so ready, so tight and wet," he muttered.

Before she could tell him that *he* was the reason she was always ready, he covered her mouth with his. The kiss sucked the breath from her lungs, soft and warm and thrilling, his tongue matching the strokes of his finger. Long, deep, languid strokes. He slid another finger into her aching sex, kissing her, murmuring encouraging pleas against her lips, and then his thumb circled her clit and she exploded.

She cried out against his mouth, rocked against his fingers, her mind nothing but a big pile of mush while her body convulsed.

When she finally came back down to earth, she found Brody watching her with surprising tenderness. "You're gorgeous, Hayden," he murmured, withdrawing his fingers and fixing her dress.

Her heart squeezed. She opened her mouth to thank him— for the compliment, the orgasm, the shoulder to lean on— but he didn't give her the chance. "Will you let me come home with you tonight? No big deal if you say no. I just, uh, thought I'd ask."

He was so polite, so careful, when the heat in his eyes and his unsteady breathing told her he'd probably die from arousal if she said no. But it touched her that he'd asked instead of assumed.

"If we go to the penthouse," she began slowly, "what exactly will we do?"

A sensual twinkle filled his eyes. His voice lowered to a husky pitch as he said, "Well, I noticed there's a removable showerhead in the master bathroom."

She burst out laughing. "Do you make it a habit of scoping out the shower when you use other people's bathrooms?"

"Who doesn't?"

9

A FEW DAYS LATER Hayden was standing outside the lavish ten-bedroom home her father had bought for Sheila. It was only a few blocks from the Gallagher Club, in the heart of one of the wealthiest neighborhoods in Chicago.

Hayden had finally decided to talk to Sheila to learn more about her father's drinking problem. Although a part of her still didn't fully trust her stepmother, she knew this conversation was long overdue. If she had more information, maybe she could find a way to help her dad. And if his recent behavior was any indication, her father definitely needed some help.

Sheila answered the door wearing sweats, her expression clearly conveying her surprise at seeing her soon-to-be-ex-stepdaughter standing on the pillared doorstep.

"Hayden…what are you doing here?"

She fumbled awkwardly with the strap of her leather purse. "I think we should talk."

With a nod, Sheila opened the door wider so Hayden could step inside. The enormous front parlor, with its sparkling crystal chandelier, was as intimidating as it had been the first time she'd seen it. The white walls were devoid of artwork, a sight that made her frown. She'd encouraged her father to pick up pieces at auctions she had recommended, but it looked as if he hadn't bothered.

"So what's on your mind?" Sheila asked after they'd entered the living room.

Hayden sat on one of the fluffy teal love seats, waited for Sheila to sink down on the matching sofa, then cleared her throat. "I want you to tell me about my father's drinking."

Her stepmother raked one delicate hand through her blond hair, then clasped her hands together in her lap. "What do you want to know, Hayden?"

"When did he start?"

"Last year, about the same time the pharmaceutical company he'd invested in went bankrupt. He lost a lot of money, tried to recoup it by making more investments, and lost that, too."

Hayden fought back a wave of guilt, realizing that she'd had no idea any of this had been going on. Her father had always sounded so jovial on the phone, as if he had no cares in the world.

Was she a terrible daughter for not seeing through the lies?

"He didn't want to worry you," Sheila added as if reading her mind.

"So that's when he started drinking?"

Her stepmother nodded. "At first it was just a drink or two in the evenings, but the worse the situation got, the more he drank. I tried talking to him about it. I told him the drinking was becoming a problem, but he refused to hear it. That's when…" Sheila's voice drifted.

"That's when what?"

"He went to bed with another woman."

A silence fell between them, but this time Hayden didn't try to defend her father. That day at the law office, she'd believed Sheila to be a heartless lying bitch, accusing Pres of adultery, but after his blowup at the Gallagher Club, Hayden couldn't deny her dad had a problem. And if that problem had driven him to cheat, she needed to accept it. No point sticking her head in the sand and pretending things were okay, when they obviously weren't.

So she leaned back and allowed Sheila to continue.

"He told me what he'd done the next morning, blamed me for his infidelity, said my constant nagging forced him to do it." Sheila made an exasperated sound. "And he kept denying he had a drinking problem. I might have been able to forgive him for the affair, but I couldn't look away while he destroyed the life we'd built."

"What happened?"

"I confronted him again, ordered him to get help for his alcohol problem."

"I take it he didn't agree."

"Oh, no." Sheila's pretty features twisted in distress and anger. "He only got worse. A couple nights later, I came home from the gym and found him in the study, drunk out of his mind. That's when he confessed about the games he'd fixed."

A rush of protectiveness rose inside her. "It could have been the alcohol talking. Maybe he didn't know what he was saying."

"He knew." Her stepmother offered a knowing look. "And what he said was confirmed to me by a player on the team."

"The one you're sleeping with?" Hayden couldn't help cracking.

Two red circles splotched Sheila's cheeks. "Don't judge me, Hayden. I may have turned to another man, but only after your father betrayed me. Pres pushed me away long before I did what I did."

Her mouth closed. Sheila was right. Who the hell was she to judge? What happened within a marriage wasn't anybody's business but the people who were married, and she couldn't make assumptions or draw conclusions about a situation she hadn't been a part of.

And if she were to draw conclusions, it startled her to realize she actually believed Sheila. She might not approve of Sheila's contesting of the prenup or love for all things luxurious, but Hayden couldn't bring herself to brush off what her stepmother had told her.

If her father had really bribed players, what would happen to him if—when?—the investigation revealed the truth? Would he get off with a fine, or would she be visiting him in prison this time next year? Fear trickled through her, settling in her stomach and making her nauseous.

With a sympathetic look and a soft sigh, Sheila said, "Things aren't always as they seem. *People* aren't always as they seem." She averted her eyes, but not before Hayden saw the tears coating her lashes. "Do you want to know why I married your father, Hayden?"

For his money?

She quickly swallowed back the nasty remark, but Sheila must have seen it in her eyes because she said, "The money was part of it. I know, you probably won't understand, but I didn't have a lot of financial security growing up. My parents were dirt-poor. My father ran off with what little money we did have, and I was working by the time I was thirteen." She shrugged. "Maybe I was selfish for wanting a man who could take care of me, for wanting some security."

Sheila paused, shaking her head as if reprimanding herself. "But the money wasn't the only reason. If it was, I would have married one of the many rich jerks who showed up at the bar I waitressed at, pinching my ass and trying to get me into bed. But I didn't marry one of those guys. I married your dad."

"Why?" Hayden asked quietly, strangely fascinated by her stepmother's story.

"Because he was one of the good guys. I wasted so much time on the bad boys, the guys who light your body on fire but end up burning you out in the end. I was sick of it, so I decided to find myself a Mr. Nice—a decent, stable man who might not be the most exciting man in the world but who'd always be there for me, always put me first, financially and emotionally."

A wave of discomfort crested in Hayden's stomach, slowly rising inside her until it lodged in her throat like a wad of old chewing gum. She'd never thought she'd have anything in common with this woman, but everything Sheila had just said mirrored the thoughts Hayden had been having for years now. Wasn't that why she'd chosen Doug—because he was nice, decent and stable? Because he'd always put her first?

"But nice men aren't necessarily the *right* men," Sheila finished softly. "Nice men make mistakes, too. They can take you for granted and they can play with your emotions, just like those bad boys I wanted so badly to get away from."

She swiped at the tears staining her cheeks and lifted her chin. "Your father hurt me, Hayden. If he'd truly loved me, he would've seen that I was only trying to help him, that I wanted to be there for him the way I thought he'd be there for me. But he wasn't there for me. I feel awful about not being able to get him help for the drinking, I really do, but I couldn't take the way he was treating me. He went to another woman, he lied about his criminal actions, and now he's making me out to be a selfish gold digger."

With a bitter smile, Sheila leaned forward and stared at her with sad blue eyes. "How's that for Mr. Nice?"

HAYDEN LEFT with no real idea how to help her dad with his drinking problem, even more concerned about his possible criminal activities. She was just as confused and upset as she'd been when she'd rung the doorbell. Her cell phone rang the second she got into her car, and just when she thought this day from hell couldn't get any worse, it did. The number flashing on the phone's screen belonged to Doug.

Oh, God, she couldn't deal with this right now. But she couldn't keep avoiding her issues any longer, either. Today she'd finally opened her eyes to the downward spiral of her father's life, started to accept that her father might have become an alcoholic, adulterer and criminal.

Maybe it was time to face the other man in her life. She'd called Doug back last week, but she'd phoned in the afternoon knowing he would be in a seminar for one of the summer courses he was teaching. Maybe it made her a chicken but she hadn't been ready to talk to him yet, opting instead to leave a brief message on his machine.

She hadn't mentioned Brody in the message, either, mostly because the thought of telling Doug about Brody—on his answering machine no less—had made her palms grow damp. It would've been one thing if the situation with Brody hadn't gone beyond that first night, but it had. It'd been over a week since she'd approached him in the bar, and somehow, during that time, her casual fling had... changed.

She couldn't pinpoint when the change had occurred. All she knew was that since they'd gone skating after the Gallagher Club party, she and Brody had been having fun not only in the bedroom, but out of it. They'd gone back to the Lakeshore Lounge for dinner, gone skating at Millennium Park. Brody had even taken her to the Art Institute of Chicago, where he'd spent the entire day following her from painting to painting and listening to her rave about each one.

What *wasn't* fun, however, was having him fly to another city every other day. He'd had three away games this past week and each time he'd left to catch his flight she'd had to bite her tongue. Had to remind herself that no matter how much she was enjoying being with Brody, this was still a fling. And flings always came to an end at some point.

Her phone continued to chime, the ring tone speeding up to signal that voice mail would kick in soon.

Hayden took a deep breath.

She had to pick up. Doug had already left her three messages since she'd called him back, his voice growing more and more concerned with each call. He probably thought she was lying dead in a ditch somewhere, and she was disgusted with herself for her inability to deal with this Doug dilemma.

No more stalling. She'd already endured one unwanted confrontation today. Might as well make it two for two.

She hit the talk button on her cell phone.

"Thank God," Doug said when she answered. "I was beginning to think something terrible had happened to you."

His obvious relief caused guilt to buzz around in her belly like a swarm of angry wasps. She felt like total slime for making him worry like this.

"Don't worry, I'm fine," she replied, her fingers trembling against the phone. "Didn't you get my message?"

"I got it, but I've called you a few times since, Hayden."

"I know. I'm sorry I didn't return your calls. Things have been hectic."

"I can imagine." He paused. "Some of the papers here are running stories about your father, honey."

"Yeah, it's happening here, too. I'm starting to get worried," she admitted.

Confiding in him came as naturally as brushing her teeth in the morning. She'd always been able to talk to Doug about everything. Whether it was problems at the university or something as minor as a bad haircut, he was always there to listen. It was one of the things she liked about him.

Liked.

The word hung in her mind, making her tap one hand against the steering wheel. She *liked* everything about this man. His patience, his tenderness, his generosity. And she was certain that once he finally decided the time was right for them to get physical, she'd like that, too. And that was the problem. She wasn't sure she could spend the rest of her life with a man she simply *liked*. Sure, sometimes love took time to develop, feelings could grow, friends could realize they were soul mates…at least that's what she'd always believed.

After meeting Brody, she was starting to reconsider.

She didn't just *like* sleeping with Brody. The sex was wild, passionate, all-consuming. When Brody kissed her, when he wrapped those big muscular arms around her, the ground beneath her feet fell away, her body sizzled like asphalt in a heat wave, and her heart soared higher than a fighter jet.

When Doug kissed her…none of those things happened. His kisses were sweet and tender, and she really did *like* them—damn, there was that word again.

"Honey, are you there?"

She forced her mind back to the moment, to this conversation she'd been putting off for too long. "Sorry, I just spaced out for a second. What were you saying?"

"I want to come visit you."

She nearly dropped the phone. "What? Why?"

There was an annoyed pause. "Because I miss you." Another beat, this time strained. "I was hoping maybe you missed me, too."

"I…" She couldn't bring herself to lie, but she couldn't quite tell the truth, either.

Fortunately, Doug continued speaking. "I keep thinking about what you said before you left, Hayden. I know you asked for space, but…" A heavy breath resonated from the other end of the line. "I think space will only lead to distance, and the last thing I want is distance between us. Maybe if I come out there, maybe if we sat down together and talked this through, we could figure out why you're feeling the way you are."

"Doug…" She searched for the right thing to say. Was there even a right thing? "This is something I need to figure out on my own."

"I'm part of this relationship, too," he pointed out.

"I know, but…"

Tell him about Brody.

Damn it. Why did her conscience have to chime in right now? She already felt terrible enough, sleeping with a man a few short weeks after telling her boyfriend she needed space. Could she really confess her sins, *now,* when Doug was so eager to patch things up between them?

You don't have a choice.

As much as she wanted to fight her conscience, she knew that little voice was right. She couldn't hide something this important from him. He needed to know. No, he *deserved* to know.

"I've been seeing someone," she blurted out.

Dead silence.

"Doug?"

A muffled cough sounded from the other end. "Pardon me?"

"I'm seeing someone. Here, in Chicago." She swallowed. "It's only been a couple of weeks, and it's nothing serious, but I think you should know."

"Who is he?"

"He's… It doesn't matter who he is. And I want you to know that I didn't plan on this. When I asked for space, the last thing I wanted was to jump into another relationship—"

"Relationship?" He sounded distressed. "I thought you said it wasn't serious!"

"I did. I mean, it's not." She tried to control her voice,

feeling so unbelievably guilty it was hard to get out the next words. "It just sort of…happened."

When he didn't say anything, she hurried on. The pretzel of guilt in her chest tightened into a vise around her heart. "Are you still there?"

"I'm here." He spoke slowly, curtly. "Thank you for telling me."

Her throat tightened. "Doug…" She trailed off, not sure what to say. Not sure there was anything else *to* say.

"I have to go, Hayden," he said after a long pause. "I can't talk to you right now. I need time to digest all this."

"I understand." She gulped, bringing much-needed moisture to her arid mouth. "Call me when you're ready to…"

To what? Forgive her? Yell at her?

"To talk," she finished awkwardly.

He hung up without saying goodbye, and she sat there for a moment, listening to the silence before her cell phone finally disconnected the call. She shoved the phone back into her purse and leaned against the plush driver's seat, raking both hands through her hair.

Between Sheila and Doug, she felt as if she'd spent the afternoon waving a red flag in front of a bull determined to gore her to pieces.

At least nobody could call her a coward.

10

THE ATMOSPHERE in the locker room was subdued, the usual pregame chatter absent as the players changed into their gear and spoke in hushed voices to one another. Brody would've liked to blame the serious mood on nerves; the series was 3–2, and if they won tonight's game they'd move on to the second round of play-offs. But he knew it wasn't the pressure that was weighing everyone down.

Fifteen minutes earlier, a league executive had informed the team that an investigation into the bribery claims was officially under way. Players would be interviewed privately throughout the week, and if the allegations bore any weight, proper disciplinary actions would be taken.

And possible criminal charges executed.

Lacing up his skates, Brody glanced discreetly over at Craig Wyatt, who was adjusting his shin pads. Wyatt hadn't spoken one word since the announcement, his sharp features furrowed with silent concern, his big body moving clumsily as he dressed. He was definitely worried about something.

Damn, winning this game tonight was going to be seriously tough. The morale was lower than the murky depths of the ocean, the players behaving as if individual axs were hovering over their heads.

Which one of them had taken a bribe? And was it only one? For all he knew, half the guys could be involved. The notion caused his blood to boil. You had to be a real son of a bitch to deliberately throw a game. The media had claimed only one or two games had been fixed, and early in the season, but it didn't matter to Brody when or how many. All it took was one game. One game could be the difference between making the play-offs and ending the season in defeat. It was a good thing they'd played well enough to make up for those early losses.

"Let's give them hell tonight," Wyatt said quietly as everyone began shuffling out of the locker room.

Give them hell? That was the big pep talk for the night?

From the wary looks on the other men's faces, Wyatt's words of encouragement were about as effective as dry glue.

"Craig, wait a second," Brody said, intercepting the team captain before he could exit the room.

"We've got a game to play, Croft."

"It can wait. I just need a minute."

The captain tucked his helmet under his arm. "Fine."

What now? Did he come out and ask Wyatt about the bribery bullshit? Bring up the affair with Sheila Houston?

Brody realized that maybe he should've come up with a game plan before he initiated this conversation.

"Well?" Wyatt said, looking annoyed.

He decided to take a page out of his mom's policy book: honesty. "I saw you with Sheila at the arena last week."

Wyatt's face went ashen. Then he swallowed. "I don't know what you're talking about."

"Don't bother with denial. I *saw* you." The collar of Brody's jersey suddenly felt hot and the padding underneath his uniform became tight. Sucking in a breath, he added, "How long have you been having an affair with Presley's wife?"

The air in the locker room grew tense, stifling. Wyatt's face was still white, but his eyes flashed with anger and indignation. Shoving his helmet onto his head, he shot Brody a frown. "This is none of your business."

"It is if you're the player who came forward and confirmed Sheila's accusations."

A long silence fell, dragging on too long for Brody's comfort. Wyatt's face was completely devoid of emotion, but it didn't stay that way for long. After several more beats, a look of weary resignation clouded Wyatt's eyes.

"Fine. You win. It was me." The captain's large hands trembled as he fumbled to snap his helmet into place. "I went to the league, Brody. I'm the reason this damn investigation is starting up."

Brody swallowed. His gut was suddenly burning, but he couldn't figure out if he felt angry, betrayed or relieved. He studied Wyatt's face and quietly asked, "How did you know Sheila was telling the truth?"

"I had my suspicions at the beginning of the season, when we lost a couple of games we had no business losing. And Sheila confirmed it."

Wyatt exhaled slowly, his breath coming out shaky. "I can't play on the same team as a few assholes that would sabotage us for money. I can't play for an owner who is willing to cheat."

Brody couldn't help but believe him. Wyatt seemed legitimately torn up about all this.

"You know who took the bribes then?" Brody asked.

Wyatt quickly averted his eyes. "Just drop it, Brody. Let the league conduct its investigation. You don't want to get involved in this."

"Wyatt…"

"I'm serious. It'll all get cleared up eventually. Just…drop it," he said again. Wyatt stepped toward the door. "Now get your ass out there. We've got a game to win."

Brody watched the other man stalk off. A part of him

wanted to run after Wyatt and shake some names out of the guy, but another part was telling him to let it go. Trying to force Wyatt to confide in him wouldn't achieve anything. Craig would just get angrier, more volatile, and the last thing Brody wanted to do was piss him off. Wyatt was a gifted athlete, one of the best in the league, and with play-offs happening, Brody wanted the Warriors captain focused on the game, not personal junk.

And he needed to focus on the game, too. Lately he'd spent too much time worrying, doubting his fellow players, wondering if his career would be blown to hell by the scandal. He had the truth on his side, the knowledge that he'd played clean and hard all season, but that didn't mean squat. Guilty by association, or whatever the hell they called it.

He would be a free agent in a few months, but another franchise might be loath to pick him up knowing he'd been investigated for bribery. All he could hope was that the investigation was quick, painless, and that his name wouldn't be dragged through the mud for something he hadn't done.

Cursing softly, he left the locker room and headed down the hallway leading out to the Warriors bench. As he entered the arena, the deafening cheers of the crowd assaulted his eardrums. The Lincoln Center was filled to capacity tonight, the bleachers a sea of silver and blue. Seeing the fans supporting the team by donning their jersey warmed Brody's heart, but it also renewed his anger.

All these fans who'd come out here tonight—the people yelling words of encouragement, the kids clapping their hands wildly—deserved a team they could be proud of.

Unfortunately, there was very little to feel proud about, especially when ten minutes into the first period the Warriors were already down by two goals.

And it was one of those games that went from bad to worse.

The Vipers cleaned the ice with the Warriors. By the second period, Brody was drenched in sweat, gasping for air and wanting to bodycheck everyone from the ref to his coach. It didn't even seem to matter how fast they skated, how many times they rushed the net, how many bullets they slapped at the Vipers' goalie. The opposing team was faster, sharper, better. They had the advantage of good morale on their side.

When the third period rolled around, Brody could tell most of his teammates had given up.

"This game blows," Becker sighed once they'd sunk down onto the bench after a line change.

Brody squirted a stream of water into his mouth then tossed the bottle aside. "Tell me about it," he muttered.

"So did you take the advice I gave you?" Becker asked, his eyes still on the game in front of them.

"Advice?"

"About staying away from Presley's daughter," Becker reminded him.

Stay away from Hayden? Brody almost laughed out loud. He was tempted to tell his friend that at the moment he was doing everything in his power to stay *close* to her. And he was succeeding. For the most part, anyway.

No matter how often Hayden called their relationship a fling, Brody couldn't view anything between them as casual. For the first time in his life, he was with a woman he actually liked hanging out with. Sure, he liked the sex, too—fine, he *loved* the sex—but there had been moments during the past week when he was shocked to realize there were other things he enjoyed just as much. Such as watching art documentaries with her. Holding her while she slept. Teaching her to ice-skate even though she wasn't much of a student.

She was funny and smart and her eyes lit up when she talked about something she loved. And it troubled him how that light left her eyes whenever an away game came up. He'd had to leave town three times this week, and although Hayden never said a single word about it, he could tell it bothered her. But he had no idea how to make it better, short of retiring from hockey—and he wasn't about to do that.

Yet he had to do something. Hayden seemed determined to keep him at a distance, at least when it came to admitting they were in a relationship, and he desperately wanted to bridge that gap, make her realize just how important she was becoming to him.

"Are you even listening to me?" Becker's loud sigh drew him out of his thoughts.

Brody lifted his head. "Huh? Oh, right, Pres's daughter. About that… As much as I value your advice, I…I can't stay away from her, man." He shrugged sheepishly. "I'm seeing her tonight, in fact."

Becker frowned, but before he could respond, the ref's whistle pierced the air and both men looked over to see who'd taken a penalty. Wyatt. Big surprise there.

There was no more time for chatting as Stan tossed them both back onto the ice for the penalty kill, and although Becker scored a ridiculously incredible shorthanded goal, it wasn't enough. The buzzer went off indicating the end of the third period and the game. The final score was a pathetic 5–1, Vipers.

IT DIDN'T TAKE a genius to figure out the Warriors had lost the game. Hayden could see it on every face that left the Lincoln Center. Her father was probably dreadfully disappointed.

She was tempted to go up to the owner's box and offer some sort of condolences, but she was in no mood to see her dad right now. If she were, she'd be inside the arena instead of loitering in the parking lot and waiting for Brody.

She leaned against the back of his SUV and scanned the

rear entrance of the building, willing him to come out. God, this day had been hell. Listening to Sheila's awful tale of Presley's drinking, hearing Doug's heart break on the other end of the telephone line. She didn't want to think about any of it anymore. That's why she'd left the penthouse and driven over here. The need to see Brody and lose herself in his arms was so strong she'd been willing to wait for over an hour.

When he finally emerged from the building she almost sobbed with relief. And when his midnight-blue eyes lit up at the sight of her, she wanted to sob with joy. Maybe their lives didn't mesh, maybe their careers were colossally different and their goals weren't aligned, but she couldn't remember the last time a man had looked so happy to see her.

"Hey, this is a surprise," he said, approaching her.

"Hi." She paused. "I'm sorry about the game. Does this mean the team is out of the play-offs?"

"No, the series is tied. We've got another chance to win it tomorrow."

"That's good."

For some reason, she couldn't tear her eyes from him. He looked good tonight. His hair was damp, his perfect lips slightly chapped. He'd confessed to licking them too much during games and the first time she'd seen him rubbing on lip balm she'd almost had a laughter-induced coronary. But she liked moments like that, seeing Brody out of his manly man element.

Tonight, though, he was all man. Clad in a loose wool suit that couldn't hide the defined muscles underneath it. The navy-blue color made his eyes seem even brighter, more vivid. Brody had told her that with play-offs around the corner, the league expected the players to look professional on and off the ice and, she had to admit, she liked seeing him in a suit as much as she enjoyed his faded jeans and ab-hugging T-shirts.

Unable to stop herself, she stood on her tiptoes and planted a kiss square on his mouth.

"What happened to not being seen together in public?"

She faltered, realizing this was the first time they'd ever engaged in a public display of affection and startled that she'd been the one to initiate it. "I…had a bad day" was all she could come up with.

Brody grinned. "That's all it takes for us to come out of the closet, you having a bad day? Damn, I should've pissed you off a long time ago." His expression sobered. "What happened?"

"I'll tell you all about it later. Let's get out of here first."

"Meet you at the hotel?"

She was about to nod when something stopped her. "No. How about we go to your place tonight?"

He seemed baffled, and she honestly couldn't say she blamed him. Since she'd agreed to explore this…thing…between them, they'd been doing things her way. Brody had asked her over to his house a dozen times but she'd always convinced him to stay at the penthouse instead. She'd felt that being on her own turf, sticking to familiar surroundings, would stop things from getting more serious than she wanted.

Yet suddenly she found herself longing to see Brody's house, to be with him on *his* turf.

"All right." He unlocked the door of his SUV. "You want to follow me in your car?"

"Why don't we just take yours? We can come back for my rental tomorrow."

His eyebrows soared north again, while his jaw dipped south. "You're just full of surprises tonight, aren't you? You do realize your father will see your car in the lot and know you didn't go home?"

"I don't live my life to please my dad." She sounded more bitter than she'd intended, so she softened her tone.

"Let's not talk about him. All I want to think about tonight is you and me."

He gently tucked an unruly strand of hair behind her ear. "I like the sound of that."

The drive to Brody's Hyde Park home was a short one. When they pulled up in front of his place, Hayden was pleasantly surprised to see a large Victorian with a wraparound porch and a second-floor balcony. Flowers were beginning to bloom in the beds flanking the front steps, giving the house a cheerful, inviting air.

"Weren't expecting this, were you?" he said as he shut off the engine.

"Not really." She smiled. "Don't tell me you actually planted all those flowers yourself?"

"Heck no. I didn't choose the house, either. My mom flew out here when I was drafted by the Warriors, and she found the house. She did all the gardening, too, and she visits once a year to make sure I haven't destroyed her handiwork."

They got out of the car and drifted up the cobbled path toward the front door. Inside, Hayden's surprise only grew. Decorated in warm shades of red and brown, the interior boasted a roomy living room complete with a stone fireplace, a wide maple staircase leading upstairs and an enormous modern kitchen with two glass doors opening onto the backyard.

"Want something to drink?" he offered, crossing the tiled floor toward the fridge. "I don't have that herbal tea you like, but I can brew you a cup of Earl Grey."

"How about something stronger?"

He gave a faint smile. "You really did have a bad day, didn't you?"

He moved to the wine rack on the counter and chose a bottle of red wine. Grabbing two glasses from the cupboard over the sink, he glanced over his shoulder. "Are you going to tell me about it or do I have to tickle it out of you?"

"Hmm." She chewed on her bottom lip. "I'm kind of leaning toward the tickle." Her expression sobered when he shot her an evil look. "Fine, fine… I'll tell you."

Brody poured the wine, handed her a glass and then led her to the patio doors. The backyard was spacious, adorned with more flowers that Brody's mom must have planted. The fence surrounding the area was so high she couldn't see the neighboring yards, not even from the raised deck on the patio. At the very far corner of the lawn stood an idyllic-looking gazebo surrounded by thick foliage.

They stepped onto the deck, where a surprisingly warm breeze met them. It was a gorgeous night, the warmest she'd experienced since coming home, and she breathed in the fresh air and tilted her head to admire the cloudless sky before finally releasing a long breath.

"I paid a visit to my stepmother today," she said.

She filled him in on the details, leaving her conversation with Doug for the end. Brody's jaw tensed at the mention of Doug's name, but as he'd promised her that night they'd skated at the arena, he didn't freak out about it. When she'd finished, he set his wineglass on the wide rail ringing the deck and gently caressed her shoulders.

"You didn't have to tell him about us," he said.

The remark surprised her. "Of course I did. I told *you* about *him*. Doesn't he deserve the same courtesy?" She lifted her glass to her lips.

"You're right." He paused. "So it's over between you and Doug?"

"Yes," she admitted. "He hung up on me, which is very uncharacteristic of him. I don't think he's happy with me at the moment."

When Brody didn't answer, she put down her wine and reached up to cup his strong chin with her hands. "You're not happy with me, either, are you?"

He looked her in the eye and said, "I *am* happy, babe."

"You are?"

"I love being with you, Hayden." He blew out a ragged breath. "And I'm glad it's over with Doug. It was frustrating sometimes, knowing there was another man in your life. And not just any man, but a man who works in your field, who shares your passion for art and is probably much better at those intellectual conversations you're always trying to have with me. I feel like a dumb oaf in comparison."

A pained look flashed across his handsome face, and it took her a moment to realize it wasn't really pain she saw in his eyes, but vulnerability. The idea that Brody Croft, the most masculine man she'd ever met, could be vulnerable stole the breath from her lungs. God, did he actually feel inadequate? Had *she* made him feel that way?

Her heart squeezed at the thought and she found herself reaching for him. She twined her arms around his strong, corded neck and brushed her lips over his. "You're not a dumb oaf," she murmured, running her fingers over the damp hair curling at the nape of his neck.

"Then you won't mind if I make an intelligent, rational point about how difficult you're being."

She raised her chin. "And what on earth am I being difficult about?"

Brody let out a breath. "Come on, Hayden, you think I don't see that look in your eyes whenever I have a plane to catch? Every time I left town this week you withdrew from me. I felt it."

Discomfort coiled inside her belly, causing her to drop her arms from his neck. Why was he bringing this up?

"See, you're doing it again," he pointed out, smiling faintly.

"I just…" She inhaled slowly. "I don't see why it's an issue."

"If it keeps you from entering into a relationship with me, then it *is* an issue."

A tiny spark of panic lit up inside her. "We agreed to keep things casual."

"*You* agreed to keep an open mind."

"Trust me, my mind is very open."

"Your heart isn't." His tone was so gentle she felt like crying.

She drifted over to the railing, curling her fingers over the cool steel. Brody moved so they were standing side by side, but she couldn't look at him. She knew exactly where this conversation was going, and she had no idea how to proceed.

"I think we have something really good here," he said quietly, resting his hand on hers and slowly stroking her knuckles. "You've got to admit we're good together, Hayden. Sexually, sure, but in other areas, as well. We never run out of things to talk about, we enjoy each other's company, we make each other laugh."

She finally turned her head and met his eyes. "I know we're good together, okay?"

It was incredibly hard admitting it, but it was the truth. Brody made her body sing, he made her heart soar, and she couldn't imagine any other man doing that. But she also couldn't imagine them ever having a stable life together.

"But I want someone I can build a home with." Tears pricked her eyelids. "I want to have kids, and a white picket fence, a dog. I did the whole hockey-lifestyle as a kid. I don't want to be sitting on airplanes for half the year, and when I have children, I don't want to be home alone with them while their father is gone."

He was silent for a moment. "I won't play hockey forever," he said finally.

"Do you plan on retiring soon?"

After a beat of hesitation, he said, "No."

Disappointment thundered inside her, but really, what was she expecting? That he'd throw his arms around her and say, *Yes, Hayden, I'll retire! Tomorrow! Now! Let's build a life together!*

It wasn't fair to ask him to give up a career he obviously loved, but she also wasn't willing to give up her own goals and dreams. She knew what she wanted from a relationship, and no matter how much she loved being with Brody, he couldn't give that to her.

"I wish you'd reconsider," he murmured. He shifted her around and moved closer so that his body was flush against hers. "Damn, we fit so well together."

She rubbed her pelvis against his. They did fit. Even though he was a head taller, their bodies seemed to mesh in the most basic way, and when he was inside her… God, when he was inside her she'd never felt more complete.

A soft moan escaped her lips at the delicious image of Brody's hardness filling her, and suddenly the tension of the day drained from her body and dissolved into a pool of warmth between her legs. Suddenly everything they'd just been talking about didn't seem to matter. Brody's job, her need for stability—it all faded away the moment he pressed his body to hers.

"Let's not talk anymore," she whispered. "Please, Brody, no more talking."

Her arousal must have been written all over her face because he ran his hands down her back and squeezed her buttocks. "You've got a one-track mind," he grumbled.

"Says the man who's fondling my ass," she murmured, relieved that the tension had eased. The heavy weight of the painful revelations they'd just shared floated away like a feather.

Brody bent his head and covered her mouth with his. The

kiss took her breath away, made her sag into his rock-hard chest as his greedy tongue explored the crevices of her mouth. Keeping one hand on her ass, he moved the other one to the front of her slacks, deftly popped open the button and tugged at the thin material.

Pulling back, he pushed her slacks off her body, waited for her to step out of them, then tossed them aside. Goose bumps rose on her thighs the second the night air hit her skin. She wore a pair of black bikini panties that Brody quickly disposed of.

"Your neighbors can see us," she protested when he reached for her blouse.

"Not where we're going." He quickly removed her shirt and bra, then lifted her into his arms and headed for the steps of the deck.

She wriggled in his embrace, self-conscious about her naked body being carried around in his backyard, but he kept a tight grip on her. Quickening his strides, he moved across the grass toward the gazebo, ascended the small set of stairs leading into it and set her on her feet.

Her heels made a clicking noise as they connected with the cedar floor of the little structure. She looked around the gazebo, admiring the intricate woodwork and plush white love seat tucked in the corner. When she turned back to Brody, he was as naked as she was.

She laughed. "Let me guess, sex in the gazebo is one of *your* fantasies?"

"Oh, yeah. I've wanted to do this since the moment this damn thing was built."

"What, none of your hockey groupies ever wanted to do it in the wilderness of your backyard?" she teased.

"I've never brought a woman home before."

She forced her jaw to stay closed. He'd never brought a

woman home before? The implications of that statement troubled her, but she didn't feel like dwelling on them now. As she'd said, no more talking.

At the moment, all she wanted to do was fulfill this gorgeous man's fantasy.

11

HE'D STARTLED HER with his admission. He'd seen it in Hayden's eyes the moment he'd confessed to never having brought a woman home, but fortunately that flicker of wariness had faded. Her eyes now glimmered with passion, and he loved that she wasn't complaining about the way he'd stripped her naked and carried her out to the gazebo.

Lord, she turned him on in the fiercest way. He'd sensed the untamed passion in her the moment they'd met, experienced it that first night when he'd made love to her on the hallway floor, reveled in it the night she'd tied him up to her bed and devoured his body. She was full of surprises, and he couldn't get enough of her. He loved her sass and her intelligence and her dry humor, the way she challenged him and aroused him and made him feel like more than just a hockey player.

"So what does the fantasy involve?" she asked, resting her hands on her bare hips.

He swept his gaze over her curvy body, trying to put his needs into words. He had no idea how the fantasy played out, only that his hands tingled with the urge to fondle her full, perky breasts and slip between her shapely legs.

The night breeze grew stronger, snaking into the gazebo and making his cock swell and thicken as the warm air caressed it. The wind also succeeded in hardening Hayden's small, pink nipples, which were now standing up as if demanding his attention.

But instead of reaching out to touch her, he cleared his throat and said, "Lie down on the love seat."

There was no objection. Her heels clacked against the floor as she walked over to the small couch and draped herself over the cushions. When she reached for the clasp on her right shoe he held up his hand. "Leave them on," he ordered.

"Why do men always get turned-on by a naked woman in high heels?"

"Because it's damn hot," he replied with a roll of his eyes.

"So are you just going to stand there and watch me, or do you plan to join me?"

"Eventually."

They were the same words they'd spoken to each other the night she'd admitted her taste for bondage, only this time he was the one in charge. He leaned against the railing of the gazebo and crossed his arms over his chest. "You've gotta give me some incentive, babe."

"Hmm. Like this kind of incentive?" She slid her hands to her breasts.

His breath hitched when she squeezed the lush mounds with her palms, the motion making her tits look bigger, fuller. With an impish smile, she stroked the underside of each breast, circling her nipples with her fingers and then dragging her thumbs over each hard bud.

He almost fell over backward at the sight of Hayden fondling her own breasts. His mouth was so dry he could barely swallow. He allowed her to play for a bit, then narrowed his eyes and muttered, "Spread your legs."

She did, and his breath caught in his throat again. From where he stood he could see every tantalizing inch of her glistening sex. He wanted to lick those smooth pink folds, shove his tongue inside that sweet paradise and make Hayden scream with pleasure, but he held back. His erection throbbed as he curled his fingers over his shaft.

Making slow, lazy strokes to his cock, he gave her a heavy-lidded look and said, "Touch yourself."

"Sure you don't want to do that for me?" Her voice came out throaty, so full of unbridled lust he almost came on the spot.

"Humor me," he squeezed out.

"It's your fantasy." She shrugged, grinned, and promptly lowered her hand between her legs.

Oh, man, this woman was incredible. His eyes nearly popped out of his head as she dragged her index finger down her slick folds and rubbed her swollen sex.

"That's it," he said hoarsely. "Get yourself nice and hot, Hayden."

She replied with a soft whimper. Her cheeks grew flushed the more she kept stroking herself. The hazy look in her eyes told him she was close, but her fingers continued to avoid the one place he knew would drive her over the edge.

She lifted her hand. "Brody," she murmured anxiously.

He chuckled. "Uh-uh. You won't be getting any help from me."

Agitation flickered in her eyes but still he remained on the other side of the gazebo. After a moment she gave a strangled groan and her hand returned between her thighs.

And then she came.

His hand froze over his erection. He was one dangerous stroke from a release he wasn't ready for, but for the life of him he couldn't tear his eyes from the gorgeous woman climaxing in front of him. Arching her back, Hayden cried out, moan after moan filling the warm night. Any neighbor by an open window could've heard her, but she didn't seem to care, and neither did Brody. He was a professional hockey player; his neighbors probably expected female moans of ecstasy to drift out of his house.

He leaned back against the rail and relished every moment, from the contented sighs that slipped out of her throat to the way she'd spread her legs even wider, her heels still strapped to her feet.

When she finally grew still, he crooked his finger at her. Despite the sluggishly sated look in her eyes, she stumbled from the love seat and made her way over to him.

"Has anyone ever told you you're the sexiest woman on the planet?" he murmured before dropping a kiss on her lips.

She responded with a lethargic smile. The remnants of orgasm he saw flashing across her delicate face only made him harder. Suddenly impatient, he bent down and grabbed a condom from the pocket of his jeans, then smoothed it over his throbbing shaft. Without giving her time to recover, he gripped her hips with both hands, maneuvered her around so her ass was pressed against his hard-on and drove his unbelievably stiff cock inside her damp sex.

She moaned, leaning forward and clutching at the railing with her hands. The move caused her bottom to raise, allowing him even better access. He withdrew slowly, rotated his hips the way he knew she liked, then plunged right back in to the hilt.

"This is going to be fast," he warned, his voice sounding gruff and apologetic to his ears. He wanted to make it last for her, but the way his cock kept pulsating, he knew it wouldn't be long before he toppled over that cliff into oblivion.

"I love everything you do to me. Fast, slow, hard, I don't care. Just make love to me."

The whispered reply brought a smile to his lips, but it was the phrase *make love* that caused his chest to tighten. It was the first time she'd referred to what they were doing as making love, and hearing the words brought a rush of pleasure so great his knees almost buckled.

He suddenly felt the primal need to claim this woman. Quickening his pace, he thrust into her, again and again, until his orgasm slithered down his spine, clutched at his balls, and the world in front of him fragmented in shards of light. He shuddered, palming a sweet breast with one hand while stroking the small of Hayden's back with the other, wanting to hold on to her for as long as possible.

He wrapped his arms around her from behind and nuzzled her neck, inhaling the scent of her vanilla and lavender body lotion. She gave a breathy sigh and murmured, "Your fantasies are almost as good as mine."

"Almost as good?" He laughed. "Wait until *I* tie *you* up. Then we'll see who has the hottest fantasy."

She disentangled herself from his embrace and turned to kiss him. Then she drifted to the entrance of the gazebo. "Think any of your neighbors will see me streaking through the yard?"

"*Now* you're self-conscious?"

She offered a rueful look. "I guess you're right. The whole neighborhood probably heard me, huh?"

"You are kinda loud…"

He bent down and grabbed his wool trousers, pulling them up his hips. Finding his shirt and jacket, he tucked them under his arm, walked over to Hayden and extended his arm. "Shall I walk the unclothed lady to the house?"

"You could at least let me wear your shirt."

"Nope. I want to experience the splendor of your body during this evening stroll."

"Screw strolling. I'm running."

Before he could blink she bounded down the gazebo's steps and tore across the yard, her firm ass pale in the moonlight. Laughing, he took off after her, hoping to keep her naked just a little bit longer, but she was already slipping her sweater over her head when he reached the deck.

"Spoilsport," he grumbled.

She put on her panties and slacks, then gestured to the back door. "You still have to give me a tour of the upstairs," she reminded him.

"Any room in particular you'd like to see?"

"Definitely one that features a bed. Or a removable showerhead."

With a grin, he grabbed their wineglasses from the railing and followed her inside. "Do you want more wine?" he asked.

"No, thanks."

She suddenly went quiet as he placed the glasses in the sink, and when he turned to look at her he saw her expression had grown somber.

"You okay?" he asked.

"I'm fine." She let out a breath. "I was thinking about my dad."

Brody made a face. "We just had mind-blowing sex and you're thinking about your dad?"

"It's just…the wine." She gestured to the bottle still sitting on the cedar counter. "It made me think about what Sheila told me today. You know, about my dad's drinking…" Her voice trailed, the distress in her eyes unmistakable.

"Are you going to talk to him about it?"

"Yes. No." She exhaled again. "I don't want to confront him right now, not when he's smack in the middle of this scandal."

"We're all in the middle of it now. We were told today that the investigation is under way. All the players are being interviewed this week."

Her green eyes glimmered with distress. "What kind of questions will you be asked?"

Brody shrugged. "They'll probably ask us what we know

about the allegations, try to coax confessions out of us, quiz us about whether we know if another player was involved."

"Are they going to ask about my dad?"

He nodded.

Resting her hands against the counter, she went silent for a moment, her pretty features shadowed by worry. He could tell she was upset by all of this, especially with everything she was learning about her father, and though he had no intention of making her feel worse, he unwittingly did so with his next statement.

"It was pretty much confirmed to me today that your dad fixed those games."

Her gaze rose to meet his, her mouth forming a startled *O*. "You're saying you know for sure that he did it?"

Damn. Maybe he shouldn't have spit it out the way he had, but the confrontation with Wyatt had been troubling him all night and he'd been hoping to talk it through with Hayden before the league's investigator interviewed him. He knew he'd have to tell the truth if asked, but he'd wanted her advice, wanted her to tell him how to handle the time bomb in his hands without looking like he was betraying his teammates or the team owner.

But he hadn't realized confiding in Hayden meant confirming her doubts about her father. Up until now she'd only suspected Presley had fixed those games, but with that one sentence he'd turned those suspicions into reality, and the crestfallen look on her face tugged at his insides in the most powerful way.

He wanted to comfort her, but he didn't know how.

So he kept his distance, leaned against the counter and released a slow breath. "Yes, he did it. I'm ninety-nine-percent sure of it."

"Ninety-nine percent," she repeated. "Then there's still a chance Dad wasn't involved."

"It's unlikely."

"But there's still a chance."

"Look, Hayden, I know you want to see the best in your father, but you're going to need to accept that he's probably guilty."

Her eyes widened, the color in her cheeks fading fast. "Are you going to tell the investigator that? You're going to say my dad is guilty?"

"I don't know what I'm going to say yet."

He could see her legs shaking as she walked across the tiled floor toward him. Eyes wild with panic, she placed one palm on his bare arm and tilted her head to look up at him. "You can't do it, Brody. Please, don't turn against my father."

HAYDEN DIDN'T KNOW where the words were coming from but she seemed to have no control over her vocal cords. In the back of her head she knew what she was asking of him was wrong, that if Presley was truly guilty he deserved to pay for his crimes. But this was her father, the only parent she had, the only constant in her life.

"You want me to lie?" Brody said flatly.

She swallowed. "No, I…maybe if you just didn't say anything…"

"Lying by omission is still lying, Hayden. And what if they straight out ask me if Presley bribed anyone? What do I do then?"

Desperation clawed up her throat. She knew she had no right asking him to do this for her, but she couldn't watch her father's entire life shatter before her eyes. "He's my only family," she said softly. "I just want to protect him."

Compassion flickered in Brody's eyes, but it quickly faded into annoyance. "What about me? Don't I deserve to be protected, too?"

"Your career isn't at stake," she protested.

"Like hell it isn't!" His eyes flashed. "My integrity and reputation are on the line here, Hayden. I won't throw away my career by lying to protect the team owner, not even for you."

She nearly stumbled backward, assaulted by the force of his words.

She suddenly felt so very stupid. What the hell had she been thinking, asking him to lie for her dad? Her only defense was that she *hadn't* been thinking. For a split second there, the fear seizing her insides was so strong it had overpowered her ability to think logically. Suddenly she'd been the lonely little girl who'd grown up without a mother, who didn't want to see her father carted off to jail even if it meant breaking the rules to keep him out of a cell.

What was the matter with her? She wasn't the type of woman who broke rules. And she didn't condone lies, either.

God, she couldn't believe she'd just asked Brody to throw away his honesty and honor.

With shaky steps, she walked over to him and pressed her face against his chest. She could feel his heart thudding against her ear like a drum. "I'm sorry. I shouldn't have asked you to lie. It was unfair of me to do that. I'm…" She choked on a sob. "I can't believe I just did that."

His warm hand caressed the small of her back. "It's okay. I know you're concerned about him, babe." Brody pressed a kiss to the top of her head.

"I just wish… Damn it, Brody, I want to help him."

"I know," he said gently. "But your dad is the one who got himself into this mess, and I hate to say it, but he's the one who'll have to get himself out of it."

HAYDEN'S CELL PHONE woke her early the next morning, rousing her from a restless sleep and making her groan with displeasure. She was on her side, her back pressed against Brody's big warm body, one of his long arms draped over her chest. She squeezed her eyes shut, waiting for the ringing to stop. A second of blessed silence, and then it rang again. And again. And again.

With a sigh, she disentangled herself from Brody's arms and slid out from under the covers. The sight of the alarm clock on Brody's nightstand made her grimace. Six o'clock. Who on earth was calling her this early?

"Come back to bed," came Brody's sleepy murmur.

"I will after I murder whoever keeps calling," she grumbled, padding barefoot to the armchair under the window. Her clothes and purse were draped over the chair, and she rummaged around in the pile until she found her cell.

Looking at the display, she immediately recognized Darcy's number. Uh-oh. This probably wasn't good. Not if Darcy was giving up her own beauty sleep to make a call.

Hayden flipped open the phone and said, "What's wrong?"

"Have you seen the morning paper?"

"That's what you woke me up to ask?" Hayden edged to the door, not wanting to disturb Brody. She leaned against the wall in the hallway and added, "And what are you doing up early enough to read the morning paper? Do you even subscribe to the paper?"

"I never went to bed last night." Hayden could practically see the grin on her best friend's face. "And, no, I don't get the paper. But Marco does. Marco, by the way, is my new personal trainer."

"At the rate you're going, you'll never be able to find a permanent gym, Darce." She let out a breath. "Now tell me what's so important about today's newspaper."

"You."

"Me?"

"You're in it, hon. Front page of the sports section, with your hockey player's tongue in your mouth and his hands on your ass."

She nearly choked. "You're making it up!"

"I'm afraid not."

Horror lodged in her throat. Darcy sounded serious. And if Darcy couldn't make a smart-ass remark about it, then it must be bad.

"I'll call you back in a minute," Hayden blurted, disconnecting the call.

The T-shirt Brody had given her to sleep in hung all the way down to her knees, but her arms were bare and goose bumps had risen on her skin. She wrapped her arms around her chest and hurried down the stairs two at a time. In the front hall, she unlocked the door and poked her head out, darting forward when she saw the rolled-up newspaper on the porch. The wooden floor was cool under her feet, making her shiver. Snatching up the newspaper, she headed back inside, pulling the paper from its protective plastic as she wandered into the living room.

She sank down on the couch, found the sports section, and gasped. Darcy was right. The first page boasted a large photograph of her and Brody in the Warrior arena parking lot. It must have been taken the moment she'd stood up on her toes to kiss him, and there was no mistaking it, his hands really were on her butt.

The caption read, "Warriors forward cozies up to team owner's daughter."

But it was the article beneath it that drained all the color from her face. She read it twice, not missing a single word, then set the paper on the cushion next to her and dropped her head into her hands.

"What happened?"

She jerked up at the sound of Brody's drowsy voice, to see

him standing in the doorway wearing nothing but a pair of navy-blue boxers and a concerned expression.

Without a word, Hayden pointed to the newspaper beside her. After a second of hesitation, Brody joined her on the couch and picked up the section.

She watched his face as he read the article, but he gave nothing away. Blinked a couple of times, frowned once, and finally rose slowly to his feet. "I need coffee," he muttered before walking out of the room.

Hayden stared after him in bewilderment, then shot up and rushed into the kitchen. Brody was already turning on the coffeemaker, leaning against the counter with a look of utter disbelief in his gorgeous blue eyes.

"They're saying I took a bribe," he said softly.

She moved toward him and rested her hand on his strong bicep. "It's just speculation, Brody. They don't have any proof."

"They have a *source!*" he burst out, his voice resonating with anger. "Someone actually told that reporter I took bribes from your father. This isn't a tabloid, where the so-called reporters make up sources to suit their story. Greg Michaels is an award-winning sports journalist—and someone on the team told him I took a goddamn bribe!"

Hayden's mouth went completely dry. She could barely keep up with the range of emotions flashing across Brody's face. Anger and betrayal and dismay. Shock and disgust. Fear. She wanted desperately to hold him, but his posture was so tense, his shoulders stiff, his jaw tight, every aspect of his body language screaming *back off!*

"Someone is trying to ruin me," he snapped. "Who the hell would do that? I know Wyatt is up to his ears in this mess, but I can't see him casting suspicion on me. He told me to stay out of it."

His eyes were suddenly on her, focused, sharp, as if

realizing she was in the room with him. "They think you're sleeping with me to shut me up about your father's part in it." He laughed humorlessly.

Sympathy welled up inside her, squeezing her heart like a vise. "It's going to be okay, Brody. Everything will get cleared up when you meet with the interviewer."

Another chuckle, this time laced with bitterness. "All it takes is one black mark on your name and teams look at you differently."

The coffeemaker clicked, and Brody turned his attention to it. Grabbing a mug from the cabinet over the sink, he slammed it down on the counter, filled it to the brim with coffee and swallowed a gulp of the scalding liquid, not even wincing.

Hayden had no idea what to say. How to make this better for him. So instead she just stood there, waiting, watching his face, trying to anticipate the next outburst.

But she wasn't ready for what he said next.

"I think maybe we should cool things off for a bit."

Shock slammed into her. "What?"

Setting down his mug, Brody rubbed his forehead. "I can't be dragged down along with your father," he said, so quietly she barely heard him. "If you and I are seen together, the rumors and suspicions will only grow. My career…"

He let out a string of curses. "I've worked my ass off to get to where I am, Hayden. I grew up wearing secondhand clothes and watching my parents struggle to afford anything. And finally, finally, I'm in a position to support myself, to support them. I can't lose that. I *won't* lose it."

"You're breaking up with me?"

He dragged his fingers through his hair, his eyes tortured. "I'm saying maybe we should put…us…on hold. Until the investigation concludes and the scandal blows over."

"You want to put us on hold," she echoed dully.

"Yes."

She turned away, resting her hands on the kitchen counter to steady herself. He was breaking up with her? Sorry, putting things on *hold*. Not that it made a difference. Regardless of the way he wanted to word it, Brody was pretty much telling her he didn't want her around.

Everything he'd said last night about how good they were for each other, how well they fit…what had happened to all that, huh?

The memory of the words he'd spoken only yesterday caused the bitterness swimming through her body to grow stronger. It was like a current, forcing all reason from her mind and pushing her into an eddy of resentment she knew too well. How many times had her father chosen his hockey team over her? How many times had the men in her life let their careers take the front seat while she sat in the back begging to be noticed?

"All right. If that's what you want," she said, unable to stop her tone from sounding clipped and angry. "I guess you need to look out for yourself, after all."

His eyes clouded. "Don't make it sound like that, Hayden. Like I don't give a damn about you. Because I *do* give a damn. You can't fault me for also giving a damn about everything I've worked so hard for."

She edged away from the counter, suddenly wanting to flee. Maybe it was for the best, ending it now. They'd already reached an impasse yesterday, when she'd told him his lifestyle didn't fit what she wanted in a relationship. Maybe it was better to break things off now, before it got even harder.

But although it made sense in her head, her heart couldn't stop weeping at the idea of not being with Brody.

Silence stretched between them, until Brody released a frustrated curse and raked his hands through his dark hair. "I care about you, Hayden. The last thing I want to do is end this." He shook his head, looking determined. "And I don't see it as an ending. I just want this mess to go away. I want my name cleared and my career unaffected. When it all dies down, we can pick up where we left off."

She couldn't help but laugh. "Because it's that easy, right?" Her laughter died, replaced with a tired frown. "It would have ended anyway, Brody. Sooner or later."

Anguish flooded his gaze. "Come on, don't say that. This break doesn't have to be permanent."

"Maybe it should." A sob wedged in her throat and it took every ounce of willpower she possessed to swallow it back. "We're probably doing ourselves a favor by letting go now. Maybe it will end up saving us both a lot of heartache in the future."

He opened his mouth to respond, but she didn't give him the chance. Blinking back the tears stinging her eyelids, she headed back to the bedroom to find her clothes.

12

THE CAB RIDE to the arena, where she'd left her car, was probably the most mortifying experience of Hayden's life. Somehow, while she'd gotten dressed, called the cab, murmured a soft goodbye to Brody, she'd managed to rein in her emotions. But the second she slid into the backseat and watched Brody's beautiful house disappear in the rearview mirror, she'd burst into tears.

Looking stunned, the taxi driver handed her a small packet of tissues then promptly ignored her. Despite the tears fogging her eyes she noticed the man shooting her strange looks in the mirror. Apparently it wasn't every day that a brokenhearted woman in tears rode in his cab.

And *brokenhearted* was the only word she could come up with to describe how she felt right now. Although she'd told Brody the breakup was for the best, her heart was aching so badly it felt like someone had scraped it with a razor blade. All she wanted to do was go back to the penthouse, crawl under the covers and cry.

The cab driver dropped her at the arena, where she got into her rental car, swiped at her wet eyes and took a few calming breaths.

Fifteen excruciatingly long minutes later, she was walking into the hotel, hoping nobody noticed her blotchy face. In the lobby, the clerk behind the check-in desk gestured at her. She reluctantly headed over and was surprised when he said, "There's a man waiting for you in the bar."

Hope and happiness soared inside her. Brody? He would've definitely had time to get here before her, since she'd had to pick up her car. Maybe he realized how foolish it was to end things because of something a reporter had written.

She hurried across the marble floor toward the large oak doors leading into the hotel bar. Only a few patrons were inside, and when she searched for Brody's massive shoulders and unruly dark hair, she came up empty-handed. Disappointment crashed into her like a tidal wave. Of course he wasn't here. He'd made it clear back at his place that he couldn't risk his career by being seen with her.

She glanced around again, then gasped when her attention landed on a man she'd dismissed during her first inspection.

Doug.

Oh, God. What was *he* doing here?

"Hayden!" He walked toward her with a timid smile.

She stared at him, taking in the familiar sight of his blond hair, arranged in a no-nonsense haircut. His pale blue eyes, serious as always. That lean, trim body he kept in shape at the university gym. He wore a pair of starched tan slacks and a crisp, white button-down shirt, and the conservative attire kind of irked her. Everything about Doug was neat and orderly and unbelievably tedious. She found herself longing for even the tiniest bit of disorder. An undone button. A coffee stain. A patch of stubble he'd missed while shaving.

But there was nothing disorderly about this man. He was like a perfectly wrapped gift that only used three efficient pieces of tape and featured a little bow with the same length tails. The kind of gift you hesitated to open because you'd feel like an ass messing it up.

Brody, on the other hand… Now he was a gift you tore open

the second you got it—the exterior didn't matter because you knew what it contained inside was a million times better anyway.

Tears stung her eyes at the thought.

"Hi," Doug said gently. "It's good to see you."

She wanted to tell him it was good to see him, too, but the words refused to come out. They stared at each other for a moment, and then he was pulling her into an awkward embrace. She halfheartedly hugged him back, noticing that the feel of his arms around her had no effect on her whatsoever.

"I know I shouldn't have come," Doug said, releasing her. "But after the way we left things…I thought we needed to talk. In person."

"You're right." She swallowed. "Do you want to come up?"

He nodded.

Without a word, they walked out of the bar and headed for the elevator. Silence stretched between them as they rode the car up to the penthouse. Hayden wanted to apologize to him again, and yet she wasn't sure she felt apologetic anymore. She and Doug had been on a break when she'd started seeing Brody, and though she regretted hurting Doug, she couldn't will up any regret about what she felt for Brody.

"I was shocked when you told me that you were seeing someone else," Doug began when they stepped into the suite.

"I know." Guilt tugged at her gut. "I'm sorry I just dropped it on you like that, and over the phone, but I had to be honest."

"I'm glad you were." He stepped closer, his eyes glimmering with something she couldn't put a finger on. "And it was the kick in the behind I needed, Hayden. It made me realize how much I don't want to lose you."

He reached out and tenderly stroked her cheek.

Discomfort crept up her spine.

"I love you, Hayden," Doug said earnestly. "I should have

said it a long time ago, but I wanted to go slow. I guess I was going *too* slow. I'm sorry."

He moved closer, but he didn't touch her again, or kiss her, just offered an affectionate smile and said, "I decided we've waited long enough. I want us to cross that bridge. I want us to make love."

No, not the intimacy bridge. Hysterical laughter bubbled inside her throat. "Doug—"

"It's finally the right time, Hayden."

Maybe it's the right time for you, she wanted to say. But for her, that perfect moment she might've shared with Doug had slipped away the second Brody Croft had walked into her life.

He reached out for her again, but she moved back, guilty when she saw the hurt in his eyes.

"It's not the right time," she said quietly. "And I think there's a reason we never got to this point before, Doug. I think…it wasn't meant to be."

He went still. "I see," he said, his voice stiff.

She took hold of his hand, squeezing his fingers tightly. "You know I'm right, Doug. Would you honestly be saying all of this, now, if I hadn't met someone else?"

"Yes." But his voice lacked conviction.

"I think we got together because it was comfortable. We were friends, colleagues, two people who liked each other well enough…but we're not soul mates, Doug."

Pain circled her heart. She hated saying these words to him, but there was no other choice.

Being with Brody had made her realize that she wasn't going to settle for a man just because he happened to be nice and dependable. As wild and sexy and unpredictable as Brody was, he was also honest and tender, more intelligent than he gave himself credit for, strong, funny, generous… Oh, God, had she fallen in love with him?

No, she couldn't have. Brody was just a fling. He might have some wonderful traits, but his career would constantly keep him away from her. She wanted someone safe, someone solid. Not someone who was so big and bold and arrogant and passionate and temporary and— Damn it!

She loved him. And wasn't it ridiculously ironic that she'd figured it out the day he broke up with her.

"Hayden? Please don't cry, honey."

She glanced up to see Doug's worried expression, then touched her cheeks and felt the tears. She quickly wiped them away. "Doug…I'm sorry," she murmured, not knowing what else to say.

He nodded. "I know. I'm sorry, too." He tilted his head, looking a bit confused. "But I don't see what's so wrong with comfortable."

"There's nothing wrong with it. But I want more than comfort. I want…love and passion and…I want *earth-shattering.*"

He gave her a rueful smile. "I don't have much experience in shattering a woman's world, I'm afraid."

No, but Brody did.

Unfortunately, he also had plenty of experience in shattering a woman's *heart.*

TWO DAYS LATER Hayden woke up feeling confused, devastated and angry. The anger surprised her, but most of it was directed at herself anyway. She'd tossed and turned all night, thinking about what a mess she'd gotten herself into since she'd come back to Chicago. She'd propositioned a stranger, then proceeded to fall in love with him. She'd hurt Doug. Discovered her father had a drinking problem and was probably a criminal.

And what exactly are you doing to fix any of it? a little voice chastised.

She forced herself into a sitting position, her anger escalating. What *was* she doing to fix it? She'd spent all day yesterday lying on the couch in her sweatpants. She'd watched the Warriors play the Vipers, trying to catch glimpses of Brody. And when the team had lost, her heart ached for him. The Warriors were officially out of the play-offs, and she knew how disappointed Brody must be. She'd been so tempted to call and tell him she was sorry. Instead, she'd devoured a carton of ice cream and gone to bed at ten o'clock.

How was that going to help anything? She wasn't the type to let problems pile up without looking for solutions, and although she might not be able to "fix" Doug's broken heart or Brody's decision to stay away from her, she sure as hell could do something about her father.

Jumping out of bed, she threw on some clothes, headed for the bathroom to wash up, then stepped into the elevator with renewed energy and determination.

Enough was enough. She needed to look her dad in the eye and demand the truth from him. This scandal was affecting her, too, and she deserved to know whether or not the trust and faith she'd placed in her father was justified. Presley's mess had taken her away from Doug and brought her to Chicago, it had broken up her and Brody, caused stress to tangle inside her. It was time to quit avoiding her father and try to make sense of everything that had happened.

She drove to the Lincoln Center with a heavy heart, knowing her dad was scheduled to be interviewed by the league investigator today. Come to think of it, Brody was being interviewed, too. She hoped she wouldn't run into him. If she did, she'd be tempted to hurl herself into his arms, and she had no desire to be pushed away again.

Ironic that she'd been fighting this relationship from day one, set on keeping it a fling, and in the end he'd been the one to break things off.

And she'd been the one to fall in love.

Forcing the painful thoughts from her mind, she parked the car and walked to the arena's entrance. After greeting the woman at the lobby desk, she rode the elevator up to the second floor, which housed the franchise offices.

Her father's office was at the end of the hall, through a pair of intimidating wood doors more suited for a president than the owner of a hockey team. Tucked off to the right was the desk of her dad's secretary, a pleasant woman named Kathy who was nowhere to be found.

Hayden walked up to the doors, but stopped when her dad's voice practically boomed out of the walls. He sounded angry.

She slowly turned the knob and inched open the door, then froze when she heard her dad say, "I know I promised to cover your ass, Becker, but this is getting out of hand."

Becker…Becker…hadn't Brody shown up at the Gallagher Club with a player named Becker?

Her blood ran cold. She knew she shouldn't stand there and listen, but she couldn't bring herself to announce her presence.

"I don't give a damn about that…they won't trace the money…"

Enough. She'd had enough.

Feeling sick to her stomach, Hayden pushed open the door and strode into her father's office. He was standing behind his desk, clutching the phone to his ear, and he nearly dropped the receiver when he saw her enter.

"I have to go," he said into the phone, hanging up without giving the other person—Becker?—a chance to respond.

Hayden inched closer, fighting the urge to throw up as she stared into her father's eyes. His face had gone pale, and she could see his hands trembling as he waited for her to approach.

"So it's true," she said flatly, not bothering with any pleasantries.

Her dad had the nerve to feign ignorance. "I don't know what you're talking about, sweetheart."

"Bullshit!" Her voice trembled with anger. "I heard what you said just now!"

Silence hung over the room. Her father looked stunned by her outburst. After a second, he lowered himself into his leather chair, gave her a repentant look and released a heavy sigh. "You shouldn't have eavesdropped, Hayden. I didn't want you involved in any of this."

"You didn't want me involved? Is that why you asked me to come home? Is that why you practically forced me to give a deposition in your divorce? So I wouldn't be involved? Too late, Dad. I already am."

Her legs barely carried her as she stumbled over to one of the plush burgundy visitor's chairs and sank into it. It was hard to think over the roar of her pulse in her ears. Anger and disgust and sadness mingled in her blood, forming a poisonous cocktail that seared through her veins. She couldn't believe this. The signs and suspicions had been there from the start, but hearing her father confirm his criminal actions was like a switchblade to the gut.

If someone had told her that the father she'd loved unconditionally, whose flaws she'd always ignored, whose attention she'd always craved, could be capable of such dishonesty, she would've laughed in their face. And yet it was true. Her father had broken the law. He'd lied. He'd probably cheated on his wife.

When had this man become a stranger to her?

"Honey…" He gulped. Guilt etched into his features. "At least let me explain."

"You committed a crime," she said stiffly. "What's there to explain?"

"I made a mistake." He faltered. "I made some bad investments. I…" Desperation filled his eyes. "It was only two games,

Hayden. Only two. I just needed to recover the losses, and…I…I screwed up."

Her belief in him slowly began to shatter, tiny jagged pieces of trust and faith chipping away, ripping into her insides as they sank down to her stomach like sharp little razor blades. How could he have done this? And why hadn't she seen it, damn it?

"Why didn't you call me?" she whispered.

"I was too ashamed." His voice cracked again. "I didn't want you to know I'd destroyed everything I'd built." His eyes looked so tortured Hayden had to turn away. "I never wanted another woman after your mother died. None of the ones I met even compared to her. So I focused on my job instead, first as a coach, and then as an owner. Money was tangible, you know? Something I didn't think I could lose."

When she looked at him again, she was stunned to see tears on her dad's cheeks. "But I did lose it. I lost it and I got scared. I thought I'd lose Sheila, too." He swiped viciously at his wet eyes. "I know part of the reason she married me was for my money. I'm no fool, Hayden. But Sheila and I also loved each other. Sometimes I think I still love her. She's so full of…*life,* I guess. And after so many years of feeling dead, I needed that. I didn't want to lose her. I started drinking too much, trying to forget about what was happening, I guess. Sheila tried to help me, but I wouldn't listen. I didn't want her to think I was weak…"

His voice drifted, his eyes glistening with pain, shame and unshed tears. Tears sprang to Hayden's eyes, too.

She'd never seen her father cry before. It broke her heart. And it hurt even more knowing that she hadn't even noticed while his life was spinning out of control. She knew how much his career and reputation and, yes, his wealth, mattered to him. The threat of losing it had driven him to make such hideous decisions. And she'd been so busy living her own life that she'd failed to be there for her father. Because no matter how dishonorably he'd behaved, he still was her father, and she couldn't write him off just because he'd screwed up.

She rose slowly from the chair and rounded the desk, placing her hand on her dad's shoulder. His head jerked up, his eyes wide with surprise, and then the tears flowed in earnest down his cheeks.

"I'm sorry, Hayden," he choked out.

She wrapped her arms around him and hugged him tightly. "I know you are, Daddy. Don't worry. We're going to get you some help." She swallowed. "And you're…you're going to have to tell the truth today, okay?"

Dropping her arms, she stared into her father's eyes, seeing the remorse and guilt flickering in them. After a moment, he nodded. "You're right," he whispered. "I know I need to face the consequences of my actions."

"I'm here for you, Dad. And if you want me to go to the interview with you, I will."

He shook his head. "It's something I need to do alone."

"I understand."

Her father rubbed his cheeks, then looked up at her and sighed. "Don't you think it's time for *you* to explain?"

"Explain what?" she asked in bewilderment.

"I do read the newspapers, Hayden." He shook his head. "How long have you been seeing Croft?"

Heat flooded her cheeks. "Not long."

"And this affair…you think it's a good idea? Croft isn't your usual type, sweetheart."

"It's not an affair," she blurted out. "I…I love him." She couldn't fight the tears that stung her eyelids. "I want to be with him, Dad."

She paused as the words settled between them. *I want to be with him.* And then she thought of what she'd told her father, just a moment ago. *I'm here for you.*

Why was it so easy for her to say that to her father, but not to Brody? He might not have the stable life she'd always longed for, but didn't he have so many other incredible qualities that more than made up for having to travel every now and then?

She suddenly realized how unfairly she'd treated him, wanting to keep everything on her terms. Fighting him when he tried to make her see they were good for each other.

Well, he was right. They *were* good for each other. Brody was the first man she'd ever been truly herself with. He made her laugh. He drove her wild in bed. He listened.

God, she didn't deserve Brody. All she'd done since the day they'd met was set boundaries, have expectations, find reasons why he wasn't right for her. Yet he'd stayed by her side. Even when she came up with silly rules, or told him he was nothing but a fling. Wasn't that what she claimed to want in a man? Someone solid to stand by her?

And didn't Brody deserve the same thing, a woman who stood by him? He cared about her, she *knew* he did, and if he thought putting their relationship on hold until the scandal blew over was best, maybe she needed to trust him.

She stumbled away from the desk, suddenly knowing what she had to do.

"Hayden?" her dad said quietly.

"I need to take care of something," she answered, inhaling deeply. "We'll talk after your interview, okay? We'll talk about everything."

Her father nodded.

She was halfway out the door when she glanced over her shoulder and added, "And, Daddy? I hope you remember to do the right thing."

BRODY STOOD outside the conference room, anxiously tugging at his tie as he waited. Damn, he hated this tie. It was choking the life out of him. Or maybe he found it so hard to breathe because any minute now he'd be sitting in front of three people who could very well destroy his career.

Both explanations were logical, but deep down he knew there was only one reason for the turmoil afflicting his body—Hayden.

He hadn't thought it was possible to miss someone this much. He hadn't been able to stop thinking about her from the second she'd left his house two days ago. Which was probably why his performance during that final game against the Vipers had been less than stellar. But even though the team was out of the play-offs, Brody's disappointment wasn't as great as it should have been. His season had officially ended, and yet he hardly cared. How could he, when his entire body ached for Hayden? Although his brain insisted he'd done the right thing by distancing himself from her, his heart refused to accept the decision. In fact, his heart had been screaming such vile things at him for two days now that he was beginning to feel like the biggest cad on the planet.

Had he made a mistake? He hadn't wanted a permanent break, hadn't intended to end the relationship; he'd just wanted the investigation to be done with, the scandal an unpleasant blip on his memory radar. But Hayden, well, she'd gone and made it permanent. Reverted to her belief that a relationship between them could never have lasted anyway.

Yet he couldn't bring himself to agree. She was wrong about them. If she'd only let down her guard and open her heart she'd see that the two of them could be dynamite together. Not just in bed, but in life. So he traveled for work. He'd have to retire sooner or later, and when he did, he planned on settling down in one place and opening a skating arena that didn't require a membership fee, so that kids from poorer families would have access to the same facilities as those who were better off. He might even coach a kids' team. It was an idea he'd been tossing around for years now.

But instead of planning a future with Hayden, he'd lost her. Maybe he'd never really had her to begin with….

"Croft."

He raised his head, frowning when he spotted Craig Wyatt walking toward him.

Wyatt's massive frame was squeezed into a tailored black suit, his shiny dress shoes squeaking against the tiled floor. The captain's blond hair was gelled back from his forehead.

"What's up?" Brody couldn't stop the twinge of bitterness in his voice.

A muscle twitched in Wyatt's square jaw. "I saw the article about you and Presley's daughter, Brody. You have no reason to be nervous. We both know you didn't do anything wrong."

"You're right, I didn't." He couldn't help adding, "But how did you know?"

Wyatt jerked his finger to the left and said, "Follow me. We need to have a chat."

Brody glanced at his watch, noting he had another twenty minutes before they called him in for his scheduled interview.

They walked silently toward the lobby, then exited the front doors and stepped into the cool morning air. Cars whizzed by in front of the arena. Pedestrians ambled down the sidewalk without giving the two men a second look. Everyone was going about their day, cheerfully heading to work, while Brody was here, waiting to be questioned about something he wanted no part in.

With a strangled groan, Wyatt ran one hand through his hair, messing up the style he'd obviously taken great care with. "Look, I'm not going to lie. I've been seeing Sheila, okay?" His voice cracked. "I know it's wrong. I know I have no business sleeping with a married woman, but, goddammit, I was a goner from the moment I met her. I love her, man."

"Sheila told you who took bribes, didn't she?"

Wyatt averted his eyes. "Yes."

"Then who, damn it? Who the fuck put us in this position, Craig?"

There was a beat of silence. "I don't think you want to know, man."

Another pause. Longer this time. Brody could tell that the last thing Craig Wyatt wanted to do was name names.

But he did. "Nicklaus did. And—" Wyatt took a breath. "I'm sorry, Brody, but…so did Sam Becker."

13

THE GROUND BENEATH Brody's feet swiftly disintegrated. He sagged forward, planting both hands on his thighs to steady himself. Sucked in a series of long breaths. Waited for his pulse to steady.

"Those are the only two Sheila knows about," Wyatt was saying. "There could be more."

Brody glanced up at Wyatt with anger. "You're lying. Nicklaus maybe, but not Becker. He wouldn't do that."

"He did."

No. Not Becker. Brody pictured Becker's face, thinking back to the first day they'd met, how Sam Becker had taken Brody's rookie self under his wing and helped him become the player he was today. Becker was his best friend on the team. He was a stand-up guy, a champion, a legend. Why would he throw his career away for some extra pocket money?

"He's retiring at the end of the season," Wyatt said, as if reading Brody's mind. He shrugged. "Maybe he needed a bigger nest egg."

Brody closed his eyes briefly. When he opened them, he saw the sympathy on Wyatt's face. "I know you two are close," Craig said quietly.

"You could be wrong about this. Sheila could have lied." Brody knew he was grasping at straws, but anything was better than accepting that Becker had done this.

"It's the truth," Wyatt answered.

They stood there for a moment, neither one speaking, until Wyatt finally cleared his throat and said, "We should go back inside."

"You go. I'll be there in a minute."

After Wyatt left, Brody adjusted his tie, wondering if he'd ever be able to breathe again. His head still spun from Craig's words. And yet he couldn't bring himself to believe it. Damn it, he needed to talk to Becker. Look his friend in the eye and demand the truth. Prove Wyatt wrong.

Then he looked up and realized he was going to be granted his wish sooner than he'd expected. Samuel T. Becker had just exited the arena.

Becker spotted him instantly, and made his way over. "You done already?"

"Haven't even gone in yet." He tried to mask his emotions as he studied his old friend. "Are you scheduled to be interviewed today?"

"Yep," Becker said. "And as a reward, I get to take Mary shopping afterward. What fun for me."

Brody smiled weakly.

"What the hell's up with you?" Sam demanded, rolling his eyes. "Don't tell me you're still gaga over Presley's daughter. I told you, man, you shouldn't be seeing her."

Yeah, he had told him, hadn't he? And Brody now had to wonder exactly where the advice had stemmed from. Had Becker really been looking out for him, or had he wanted to keep him away from Hayden in case Presley decided to confide in his daughter? In case Brody learned the truth about Becker's criminal actions. The thought made his blood run cold.

"Let's not talk about Hayden," he said stiffly.

"Okay. Whatcha want to talk about then?"

He released a slow breath. "How about you tell me why you let Presley bribe you?"

Becker's jaw hardened. "Excuse me?"

"You heard me."

After a beat, Becker scowled. "I already told you, I wasn't involved in that crap."

"Someone else says otherwise."

"Yeah, who?" Becker challenged.

Brody decided to take a gamble. He felt like a total ass, but still he said, "Presley."

The lie stretched between them, and the myriad of emotions Brody saw on his friend's face was disconcerting as hell. Becker's expression went from shocked to angry. To guilty. And finally, betrayed.

And it was all Brody needed to know.

With a stiff nod, he brushed past his former mentor. "I'm needed inside."

"Brody, come on." Becker trailed after him, his voice laced with misery. "Come on, it wasn't like that."

Brody spun around. "Then you didn't sell out the team?"

Becker hesitated a little too long.

"That's what I thought."

"I did it for Mary, okay?" Becker burst out, looking so anguished that Brody almost felt sorry for him. "You don't know what it's like living with a woman like her. Money, power, that's all she talks about. She's always needling me to be better, richer, more ambitious. And now that I'm retiring, she's going nuts. She married me because of my career, because I was at the top of my game, a two-time cup winner, a goddamn champion."

"And you could've retired knowing that you *are* a champion and a two-time cup winner," Brody pointed out. "Now you'll go out a criminal. How's Mary going to like that?"

Becker said nothing. He looked beaten, weak. "I messed up, kiddo, and I'm sorry," he whispered after several moments had passed. "I'm sorry about the games and the article and—"

Brody's jaw tightened. "The article?"

His friend averted his eyes, as if realizing his slipup.

Brody stood there for a moment, wary, studying Becker. The article…the one that had been in the paper two days ago? The one that featured a source who insinuated Brody had taken a bribe?

His blood began to boil, heating his veins, churning his stomach, until a red haze of fury swept over him.

"You spoke to the reporter about me," he hissed.

Becker finally met his eyes. Guilt was written all over his face. "I'm sorry."

"Why? Why the *hell* would you do that?" Brody clenched his fists, knowing the answer before Becker could open his mouth. "To take the blame off yourself. You were too close to being caught, weren't you, Sam? You thought my relationship with Hayden would get the press going, put some pressure on me instead of you."

The sheer force of Brody's anger was unbelievable. He wanted to hit the other man, so badly his fists actually tingled. And along with the rage came a jolt of devastation that torpedoed into his gut and brought a wave of nausea to his throat.

"I'm sorry," Becker murmured for what seemed like the millionth time, but Brody was done listening to his friend's apologies. No, not his friend. Because a true friend would never have done what Sam Becker had.

Without another word, he brushed past Becker and stalked into the arena.

He felt like slamming his fist into something. Becker, his best friend, had betrayed him. Becker, the most talented player in the league, had cheated. And why? For money. Goddamn *money.*

Money. Power. Ambition. She married me because of my career.

And suddenly Brody found himself sagging against the wall as the truth of his own stupidity hit him. Didn't he, too, place importance on financial success? Hadn't he just thrown away the woman he loved because of his damn career?

And, God, but he did love Hayden.

He loved her so damn much.

Maybe he'd fallen for Hayden when she'd first strolled up and proceeded to wipe the pool table with him. Or maybe it happened the first time they'd kissed. Or the first time they'd made love. It could've been the night she'd put on the pair of skates and stumbled all over the ice, or the day she'd dragged him around the museum talking passionately about every piece of art.

He didn't know when it happened, but it had. And instead of clinging to the woman whose intelligence amazed him, whose passion excited him, whose soft smiles and warm arms made him feel more content than he'd ever felt in his life—instead of hanging on to her, he'd pushed her away.

And why? Because he'd been implicated in a crime he hadn't committed? Because his family never had money when he was growing up? So what? His parents loved each other, and their marriage had thrived despite their financial difficulties. What did money and success really matter when you didn't have someone to share it with, someone you loved?

A laugh suddenly slipped out of his mouth, and he noticed the receptionist giving him a funny look. Releasing a shaky breath, he crossed the lobby toward the hallway off to the left and walked back in the direction of the conference room. Lord, he was an ass. He'd been searching for a woman who'd look at him and see past the athlete, and, damn it, but he'd found her. Hayden didn't care if he was a star and she didn't care how much money he made, as long as he was there for her.

He wasn't willing to lie to protect Hayden's father, but he should have told her he'd stand by her no matter what happened with her dad. His relationship with the team owner's daughter might place a negative spotlight on him, but wasn't it worth it if it meant keeping Hayden in his life?

"Brody?"

He almost tripped when he saw Hayden standing at the end of the hall, right in front of the conference-room door.

"What are you doing here?" he asked.

She stepped toward him, and he noticed her red-rimmed eyes. Had she been crying?

"I came to talk to my dad," she murmured. "And then I remembered that you were being interviewed, too, so I thought I'd find you before you had to go in…" Her voice drifted, and then she cleared her throat. "I'm sorry the team didn't make it to the second round."

"So am I… But to be honest, it doesn't seem all that important anymore, considering everything else that's going on."

"I know." She gave him a sad smile. "A criminal investigation kind of casts a shadow over things, doesn't it?"

The pain in her eyes tore at his insides. He hated seeing her this way, and he knew why she'd been crying.

Resting his hand on her arm, he slowly pulled her away from the conference-room door and led her to the end of the hall. "I'm not going to lie," he said softly.

She tilted her head to meet his eyes, her gaze confused, then opened her mouth to speak.

"Wait," he cut in. "I want you to know that just because I won't lie doesn't mean I won't be there for you. Because I will, babe. I don't care what the papers write about us, I don't care how my career is affected. I don't care about anything but you. I'll stay by your side, Hayden. I promise, I'll be here for you, as long as you need me."

He blew out a breath, waiting for her to reply, praying she didn't say, *Well, I don't need you, Brody. It was just a fling.*

But she didn't say that. She didn't say anything, in fact.

Instead, she burst out laughing.

HAYDEN COULDN'T STOP the giggles from escaping. She'd come down here to tell Brody she was willing to wait until the investigation ended, that she would do anything it took to keep him in her life, even if it meant staying apart for a while. And here he was, telling her he wanted to stay by her side.

"You think it's funny?" Brody said in annoyance, raking both hands through his dark hair. "Remind me never to make a grand romantic gesture again."

She chuckled. "I only think it's funny because I came to tell you I'll stay away from you until the investigation is finished."

"What?"

"I respect your decision. If you want to lie low until this blows over, I'll do that." She curled her fingers over his arm and looked at him imploringly. "But I don't want it to be permanent. I don't want us to end, Brody."

His features softened. "Neither do I." He paused. "I also don't want us to lie low."

"Are you sure?"

He moved closer, bent down and planted a soft kiss on her mouth, right there in the hallway. Then he pulled back, smiled, and dipped his head to kiss her again, this time slipping her a little tongue.

Flushed, she broke the kiss and stepped back before she gave in to the urge to pull him into the restroom and fulfill yet another kinky fantasy. "Come to the hotel when you're done," she said, her voice coming out breathy.

He grinned. "I'll be there with bells on."

"No bells. But naked would be good." Her heart did a crazy

little somersault. "And don't keep me waiting too long." She drew in a breath. "There are definitely a few things I still need to say to you."

AN HOUR LATER, Brody stepped into the elevator at the Ritz. He waited for the bellhop to turn the key that gave him access to the penthouse floor, and when the guy left, Brody sagged against the wall of the car, feeling as if he'd just run the Boston Marathon and followed that up by climbing Everest. The interview with the league investigators had been pure torture. He'd sat there in his suit, with his oxygen-depriving tie, and had had to sell out a man he'd once considered a friend and another he'd respected as a boss.

Thank God this day from hell was over. He didn't know what the investigation would turn up, how it would all end, but a load had been lifted off his chest. One load, at least. He still hadn't quite faced the fact that Becker had betrayed him. He knew it would take more than one afternoon to come to terms with it. But he'd walked out of that conference with his conscience clear, and now he couldn't wait to lose himself in Hayden's arms and forget about everything except the love he felt for her.

"Hayden?" he called as the elevator doors swung open and he entered the living room.

Her voice drifted out from the bedroom. "In here."

He found her in the bedroom, sitting cross-legged in the center of the bed, still clad in the flowy green skirt and yellow silk top she'd been wearing earlier. Damn. He'd been hoping to find her naked.

Ah, well, that could be easily amended.

She slid off the bed, her skirt swirling around her firm thighs as she moved toward him. "How was the interview?"

"Terrible. But I think I convinced them I wasn't guilty of any wrongdoing."

Relief flooded her features. "Good." Then, looking somber, she added, "I found out something about Becker that you're not going to like."

He swallowed. "I know already. Who told you?" he asked after exhaling a shaky breath.

"I overheard my dad talking to him on the phone. So it's true? He really did do it?"

"Yes." He swallowed. "Nicklaus took a bribe, too—he's our goalie." His anger returned like a punch to the gut. "I can't believe they would do that. Especially Sam."

"I'm sorry," Hayden said again, reaching up to touch his chin with her warm fingers. "But I think forgiveness will come in time. If I can forgive my dad, maybe you'll be able to forgive your friend."

Brody faltered. "And if I can't?"

"I'll help you." She smiled glibly. "I'm good at forgiveness. After all, didn't I forgive you for dumping me?"

"I panicked, okay? And I only suggested we put things on hol—" He stopped when he saw the amusement in her eyes. "You're not mad," he said.

"Of course not." She ran her index finger along the curve of his jaw. "I can't stay mad at the man I love."

He held his breath, not daring to give in to the sheer bliss threatening to spill over. "You mean that?"

"Yes." She lifted her other hand and cupped his chin with both her hands. "I love you, Brody. I know I kept fighting you whenever you said we were perfect for each other, but…I'm not fighting anymore." She exhaled slowly. "I've fallen for you, hockey star. The earth moves when we're together and I love it. I love you."

The joy in his heart spilled over, warming his insides and making his pulse skate through his veins like a player on a breakaway.

"I'm willing to be part of the hockey lifestyle for as long as it takes," she added, certainty shining in her eyes. "I'll even go to your games." She chewed on her bottom lip. "But I'll probably bring some lecture notes to work on, you know, because I still don't particularly like hockey, but I'll make an effort to—"

He silenced her with a kiss, but pulled away just as she parted her lips to let him in.

"I won't play hockey forever, Hayden," he said softly. "And I'm already trying to work on the possibility of signing with a West Coast team next season. That way you can keep teaching at Berkeley, and we could—" his voice cracked "—we could get started on building a life together. A *home*."

As he said the words, he knew without a doubt that's what he wanted. A home with Hayden. A life with the one woman who looked past his uniform and saw the man beneath it. He'd been searching for her for so long, and now that he'd found her, he wasn't about to let her go. Ever.

"I love you, Hayden," he said roughly. "More than hockey, more than being successful, more than life. I want to wake up every morning and see one of your sleepy smiles, go to bed every night pressed up against you, have kids with you, grow old with you." He put his hands on her slender hips and pulled her toward him. "Will you let me do that?"

Twining her arms around his neck, she leaned up and kissed him, a long, lingering kiss that promised love and laughter and hot, endless sex. Pulling back, just an inch, she whispered, "Yes," and then raised her lips to his again.

"Should we seal the deal?" he murmured against her hot, pliant mouth.

"God, yes."

Deepening the kiss, he untucked her shirt from the waistband of her skirt and slid his hands underneath, filling his palms with the feel of her silky skin. His tongue sought hers. His hands found her breasts.

Hayden moaned. "No, not here." Breaking contact, she darted over to the nightstand and pulled out a condom. Without another word, she grabbed his hand and dragged him out of the bedroom to the middle of the narrow hallway.

"Here," she said, a playful light dancing in her eyes.

He looked at the spot she'd chosen, chuckling when he realized this was the first place they'd made love. On the hallway floor, while Hayden writhed beneath him and squeezed his ass and pushed him into her as deep as he could go.

"Here is perfect," he answered huskily.

He drew her into his arms, claiming her with his mouth, and they were both breathless by the time the kiss ended. Gently stroking her cheek, he gave her another soft kiss, then began peeling her clothes from her body. First her shirt, then the bra, the skirt, the panties, until she was standing naked in front of him, a vision of perfection. He marveled at her silky curves and perfect skin, those beautiful breasts, the shapely legs… God, he couldn't believe she was his. All his.

"I love you, Hayden," he said, his throat thick with emotion. "I love everything about you."

She gave a soft sigh of pleasure as he cupped her breasts, tenderly stroking the swell of each perfect mound.

He hastily removed his own clothes, kicked them aside, then dropped to his knees and peppered little kisses on her flat abdomen before moving to nip at her inner thigh. He loved the sweet little moan she responded with, loved the way she tangled her fingers in his hair and guided him to the spot between her legs that he knew ached for his touch.

He kissed her sensitized nub, flicked his tongue over her sweetness. He would never be able to get enough of her, even if he spent the rest of his life trying. With a small groan, he planted one last kiss on her soft folds and then pulled her down to the carpet.

With a look of pure contentment swimming in her forest-green eyes, Hayden lay back, spread her legs and offered him a wicked smile.

"Don't keep me waiting," she said with just a hint of challenge in her throaty voice.

"I don't intend to."

He covered her body with his, his shaft, hot and hard, pressed up against her belly. He shifted so that his tip brushed her wet sex, but didn't plunge inside.

First, he kissed her again, a long, lazy kiss, and then he pulled back and said, "No ground rules this time."

Her eyelids fluttered open. "What?"

"That second night, you said there were ground rules." He nipped at the hot flesh of her neck. "No rules this time. You're getting not only my body, but my heart and my soul, every night for the rest of your life. Got it?"

She raised her brows. "Again with the demands, huh?"

"You got a problem with that?"

With a laugh, she gripped his hair with her fingers and pulled his head down. Slipping her tongue into his mouth, she kissed him until he could barely see straight, then reached between them, circled his shaft and guided it to her opening, pushing herself down over his length.

He gasped.

"I don't have…" she moaned as she took him in deeper "…a single problem with that." With a breathy sigh, she wrapped her arms around his neck and pressed a kiss to his collarbone. "I love you, Brody."

He slowly withdrew, then plunged back in, filling her to the hilt. "It drives me wild when you say that," he squeezed out.

"What, I love you?"

His cock jerked in response. "Yes, that."

She lifted her hips off the ground, and hooked her legs around his lower back, holding him prisoner with her wet heat. "Good, because I plan on saying it often. I love you, Brody Croft."

Staying true to her word, she brushed her lips over his ear and said it again. And again. And again. With a groan, he buried his head in the crook of her neck, inhaled her sweet scent and sent them both to heaven.

And when they were sated and happy and lying there on the carpet, Brody could swear that the earth had moved.

Epilogue

One year later

"SERIOUSLY, BABE, we need to do something about that shower," Brody grumbled as he stepped out of the bathroom.

Hayden couldn't help but laugh at the aggravation on his ridiculously handsome face. "The plumber will be here on Monday, *babe*. Quit getting your panties in a knot."

He strode into the recently painted master bedroom of their San Diego home, his frown deepening. "It really doesn't bother you?"

"No, Brody. It doesn't. It's just a removable showerhead, for Pete's sake. We'll live without it for a couple more days."

She rolled her eyes and rose from the bed. They'd purchased the house two months ago, at a bargain since the rambling three-story Victorian was in desperate need of renovations. So far, they'd painted every room, gutted the living room, retiled the kitchen—and Brody was worrying about a showerhead. Her husband definitely had a one-track mind. Of course, she'd known that when she'd married him.

"We should head over to the restaurant," she said, swiftly putting an end to the subject Brody refused to drop. "Darcy will be wondering where we are."

Brody snorted. "Darcy is probably having sex with one of the waiters as we speak."

She wagged her finger at him. "Be nice. She's taken a vow of celibacy, remember?"

Another snort. "Yeah, and I'm sure that'll last for, oh, ten seconds. No, make that five."

Hayden laughed, knowing he was probably right. Leopards couldn't get rid of their spots, lions weren't about to grow horns and Darcy White certainly couldn't "quit" men. But Hayden was glad her friend was finally able to take time off and visit them. Darcy was actually considering moving to the West Coast, and Hayden was avidly encouraging her friend to do so. She would love having Darcy around on a more regular basis, especially since she wouldn't be able to travel with Brody to his away games for much longer.

Although the Warriors hadn't made it far in the play-offs last season, Brody's standings had impressed the Los Angeles Vipers' general manager, who'd made him an offer, to both Hayden and Brody's relief. It put an end to the "where do we live" dilemma that had been plaguing them since the engagement. Brody signed with the Vipers, and since the commute to San Francisco had been too much for her, she'd agreed to teach courses at Berkeley during the hockey season as well as a few summer courses. The arrangement worked for both of them; the online seminars gave her the time to work on her Ph.D. at the University of San Diego, and getting to L.A. from San Diego would be easier for Brody.

They'd married in Chicago, though, deciding it was fitting to say their vows in the city where they'd met and fallen in love. Brody's parents had flown in for the wedding; Darcy had been the maid of honor, and the guests were a mixture of academics and athletes, including Brody's former captain Craig Wyatt, who'd brought Hayden's ex-stepmother. Shockingly, Wyatt and Sheila were now engaged, and Sheila was happily planning the wedding and enjoying the money she'd gotten from her divorce; she'd eventually settled for half of Presley's estate.

Hayden's dad hadn't been able to make it to the wedding—the rehabilitation facility he'd checked himself into hadn't allowed it—but he'd sent her a beautiful letter that stated how happy he was she and Brody had found love. He'd also thanked her for supporting him through everything, and Hayden had been in tears when she'd read his heartfelt words.

"Hey, you okay?"

Brody's concerned voice drew her from her thoughts. She managed a nod. "Yeah. I was just thinking about my dad."

Brody moved closer and wrapped his strong arms around her. "I know you wish he would move out here, but you can't monitor every move he makes, Hayden. He's sober now. Just have faith that he'll stay that way."

"I know." She sighed. "At least he's not in jail."

Last year's league investigation had resulted in criminal charges being brought up on her father, as well as the players he'd bribed, but Presley had gotten off with a fine and four years' probation. Since her dad hadn't been involved in a gambling ring or organized crime, he'd been lucky with his punishment. He'd lost the team, though, and Hayden knew that had been a big blow for her dad. The Warriors were now owned by none other than Jonas Quade, the man of many mistresses and that god-awful tan.

Sam Becker had wound up with probation, too, but Brody still couldn't seem to forgive his former friend. Hayden hoped that in time the two men might reconcile.

"Last time he called he mentioned he's thinking of buying a place by Lake Michigan," Brody was saying, still talking about her dad. "Did he tell you that?"

"No, he didn't mention it." She suddenly smiled, wondering if maybe there was hope for her dad after all. He might have lost the team, but he seemed much happier lately, and the two of them were on their way to regaining the close relationship they'd had when she was younger.

"I told you he used to take me fishing when I was a kid, right?" she said.

Her husband kissed her on the cheek and took her hand. "Come on, we should go."

"You're right. Darce will freak out if we don't show up soon. She's been really bitchy lately. You know, the lack of sex and all."

They headed for the doorway. "Actually, I think she'll freak out when she sees *this.*" Brody rubbed her protruding belly with his palm.

Hayden sighed. She was only five months along, and already she felt huge. "Remind me again how you knocked me up when we'd decided to wait a couple years?"

He shot her a cocky grin. "I told you. I never miss. It's my fatal flaw."

"No, your fatal flaw is not getting me the ice cream I asked for last night."

They left the bedroom and walked down their brand-new winding staircase. The floor in the front hall still needed to be laid down, but Hayden didn't care as long as the renovations were done before the baby came. She grabbed her purse from the hall table and slipped into her flat sandals.

She followed Brody out on the porch, lifting her head to the late-afternoon sun and breathing in the warm San Diego air.

"I told you why I didn't pick up the ice cream," Brody grumbled. "You've got to eat healthy, babe. You're carrying a future champion in that belly of yours. Our son needs proper nourishment."

Oh, brother. Not again.

"I only need one champion in my life, thank you very much." She shot him a sweet smile. "Our *daughter* is going to be a Nobel Prize winner."

"It's a boy," he said confidently with a charming smile of his own. "Haven't you figured out by now that I always get what I want?"

"God, you're arrogant."

"Yeah, but you like it." His grin widened. "And if it weren't for me, you'd still be hiking across some intimacy bridge—"

"I should never have told you about that!"

"And deprive me of endless bridge jokes?"

She tried to scowl but ended up laughing. "Fine. I surrender. The intimacy bridge is funny. Now let's go before Darcy really does sleep with a waiter."

Brody held her arm as they walked to the car. He opened the door for her, then rounded the vehicle and got into the driver's seat.

She stretched the seat belt over her stomach and buckled up, then tucked a strand of hair behind her ears. Suddenly she became aware of Brody watching her, and when she turned her head, her breath caught at the awe, love and passion she saw shining in his eyes.

"Have I told you today how beautiful you are?" he asked.

"Twice, actually." Warmth suffused her body. "But feel free to say it as many times as you'd like."

"Believe me, I will." He shifted closer and stroked her cheek. "You know, the happiest day of my life was when you walked up to that pool table and asked me back to your hotel."

"You're not going to tell our daughter that, are you?"

"Nah. We'll tell *our son* we met at a museum and it was love at first sight."

He cupped her jaw and ran his thumb over her lower lip, sending a wave of heat and desire through her. She could never get enough of Brody's touch, not even if she lived to be a hundred.

"Let's skip dinner," he murmured, then dipped his head to kiss her.

Her pulse raced as his tongue teased hers with long, sensual strokes.

It took all her willpower to pull back. "We can't." When he grumbled, she added, "Come on, it's one little dinner. I'll make it worth your while…"

His eyes lit up. "How?"

She laughed. "You'll just have to wait and see."

"For you, I'd wait forever. In fact, I'd do just about anything you asked." His gaze softened. "I love you that much, Mrs. Croft."

She leaned closer and brushed her lips over his. "I love you, too…so let's get this dinner over with so I can get you home and show you *exactly* how much."

Celebrate 60 years of pure reading pleasure
with Harlequin®!
Silhouette® Romantic Suspense is celebrating with the
glamour-filled, adrenaline-charged series
LOVE IN 60 SECONDS starting in April 2009.

Six stories that promise to bring the glitz of Las Vegas, the
danger of revenge, the mystery of a missing diamond,
family scandals and ripped-from-the-headlines intrigue.
Get your heart racing as love happens in sixty seconds!

Enjoy a sneak peek of
USA TODAY bestselling author Marie Ferrarella's
THE HEIRESS'S 2-WEEK AFFAIR.
Available April 2009
from Silhouette® Romantic Suspense.

Eight years ago Matt Shaffer had vanished out of Natalie Rothchild's life, leaving behind a one-line note tucked under a pillow that had grown cold: *I'm sorry, but this just isn't going to work.*

That was it. No explanation, no real indication of remorse. The note had been as clinical and compassionless as an eviction notice, which, in effect, it had been, Natalie thought as she navigated through the morning traffic. Matt had written the note to evict her from his life.

She'd spent the next two weeks crying, breaking down without warning as she walked down the street, or as she sat staring at a meal she couldn't bring herself to eat.

Candace, she remembered with a bittersweet pang, had tried to get her to go clubbing in order to get her to forget about Matt.

She'd turned her twin down, but she did get her act together. If Matt didn't think enough of their relationship to try to contact her, to try to make her understand why he'd changed so radically from lover to stranger, then to hell with him. He was dead to her, she resolved. And he'd remained that way.

Until twenty minutes ago.

The adrenaline in her veins kept mounting.

Natalie focused on her driving. Vegas in the daylight wasn't nearly as alluring, as magical and glitzy as it was after dark. Like an aging woman best seen in soft lighting, Vegas's imperfections were all visible in the daylight. Natalie supposed that was why people like her sister didn't like to get up until noon. They lived for the night.

Except that Candace could no longer do that.

The thought brought a fresh, sharp ache with it.

"Damn it, Candy, what a waste," Natalie murmured under her breath.

She pulled up before the Janus casino. One of the three valets currently on duty came to life and made a beeline for her vehicle.

"Welcome to the Janus," the young attendant said cheerfully as he opened her door with a flourish.

"We'll see," she replied solemnly.

As he pulled away with her car, Natalie looked up at the casino's logo. Janus was the Roman god with two faces, one pointed toward the past, the other facing the future. It struck her as rather ironic, given what she was doing here, seeking out someone from her past in order to get answers so that the future could be settled.

The moment she entered the casino, the Vegas phenomena took hold. It was like stepping into a world where time did not matter or even make an appearance. There was only a sense of "now."

Because in Natalie's experience she'd discovered that bartenders knew the inner workings of any establishment they worked for better than anyone else, she made her way to the first bar she saw within the casino.

The bartender in attendance was a gregarious man in his early forties. He had a quick, sexy smile, which was probably one of the main reasons he'd been hired. His name tag identified him as Kevin.

Moving to her end of the bar, Kevin asked, "What'll it be, pretty lady?"

"Information." She saw a dubious look cross his brow. To counter that, she took out her badge. Granted she wasn't here in an official capacity, but Kevin didn't need to know that. "Were you on duty last night?"

Kevin began to wipe the gleaming black surface of the bar. "You mean during the gala?"

"Yes."

The smile gracing his lips was a satisfied one. Last night had obviously been profitable for him, she judged. "I caught an extra shift."

She took out Candace's photograph and carefully placed it on the bar. "Did you happen to see this woman there?"

The bartender glanced at the picture. Mild interest turned to recognition. "You mean Candace Rothchild? Yeah, she was here, loud and brassy as always. But not for long," he added, looking rather disappointed. There was always a circus when Candace was around, Natalie thought. "She and the boss had at it and then he had our head of security escort her out."

She latched on to the first part of his statement. "They argued? About what?"

He shook his head. "Couldn't tell you. Too far away for anything but body language," he confessed.

"And the head of security?" she asked.

"He got her to leave."

She leaned in over the bar. "Tell me about him."

"Don't know much," the bartender admitted. "Just that his name's Matt Shaffer. Boss flew him in from L.A., where he was head of security for Montgomery Enterprises."

There was no avoiding it, she thought darkly. She was going to have to talk to Matt. The thought left her cold. "Do you know where I can find him right now?"

Kevin glanced at his watch. "He should be in his office. On the second floor, toward the rear." He gave her the numbers of the rooms where the monitors that kept watch over the casino guests as they tried their luck against the house were located.

Taking out a twenty, she placed it on the bar. "Thanks for your help."

Kevin slipped the bill into his vest pocket. "Any time, lovely lady," he called after her. "Any time."

She debated going up the stairs, then decided on the elevator. The car that took her up to the second floor was empty. Natalie stepped out of the elevator, looked around to get her bearings and then walked toward the rear of the floor.

"Into the Valley of Death rode the six hundred," she silently recited, digging deep for a line from a poem by Tennyson. Wrapping her hand around a brass handle, she opened one of the glass doors and walked in.

The woman whose desk was closest to the door looked up. "You can't come in here. This is a restricted area."

Natalie already had her ID in her hand and held it up. "I'm looking for Matt Shaffer," she told the woman.

God, even saying his name made her mouth go dry. She was supposed to be over him, to have moved on with her life. What happened?

The woman began to answer her. "He's—"

"Right here."

The deep voice came from behind her. Natalie felt every

single nerve ending go on tactical alert at the same moment that all the hairs at the back of her neck stood up. Eight years had passed, but she would have recognized his voice anywhere.

* * * * *

Why did Matt Shaffer leave heiress-turned-cop
Natalie Rothchild?
What does he know about the death of
Natalie's twin sister?
Come and meet these two reunited lovers and learn the
secrets of the Rothchild family in

THE HEIRESS'S 2-WEEK AFFAIR

by USA TODAY *bestselling author*
Marie Ferrarella.

The first book in Silhouette® Romantic Suspense's
wildly romantic new continuity,
LOVE IN 60 SECONDS!
Available April 2009.

REQUEST YOUR FREE BOOKS!

2 FREE NOVELS PLUS 2 FREE GIFTS!

Red-hot reads!

HB09R

You're invited to join our Tell Harlequin Reader Panel!

By joining our new reader panel you will:

- Receive Harlequin® books—they are FREE and yours to keep with no obligation to purchase anything!
- Participate in fun online surveys
- Exchange opinions and ideas with women just like you
- Have a say in our new book ideas and help us publish the best in women's fiction

In addition, you will have a chance to win great prizes and receive special gifts!
See Web site for details. Some conditions apply.
Space is limited.

To join, visit us at
www.TellHarlequin.com.

COMING NEXT MONTH

Available March 31, 2009

#459 OUT OF CONTROL Julie Miller
From 0–60
Detective Jack Riley is determined to uncover who's behind the movement of drugs through Dahlia Speedway. And he'll do whatever it takes to find out— even go undercover as a driver. But can he keep his hands off sexy mechanic Alex Morgan?

#460 NAKED ATTRACTION Jule McBride
Robby Robriquet's breathtaking looks and chiseled bod just can't be denied. But complications ensue for Ellie Lee and Robby when his dad wants Ellie's business skills for a sneaky scheme that jeopardizes their love all over again….

#461 ONCE A GAMBLER Carrie Hudson
Stolen from Time, Bk. 2
Riverboat gambler Jake Gannon's runnin', cheatin' ways may have come to an end when he aids the sweet Ellie Winslow in her search for her sister. Ellie claims she's been sent back in time, but Jake's bettin' he'll be able to convince her to stay!

#462 COMING ON STRONG Tawny Weber
Paybacks can be hell. That's what Belle Forsham finds out when she looks up former fiancé Mitch Carter. So she left him at the altar six years ago? But she needs his help now. What else can she do but show him what he's been missing?

#463 THE RIGHT STUFF Lori Wilde
Uniformly Hot!
Taylor Milton is researching her next planned fantasy adventure resort—Out of This World Lovemaking—featuring sexy air force high fliers. Volunteering for duty is Lieutenant Colonel Dr. Daniel Corben, who's ready and able to take the glam heiress to the moon and back!

#464 SHE'S GOT IT BAD Sarah Mayberry
Zoe Ford can't believe that Liam Masters has walked into her tattoo parlor. After all this time he's still an irresistible bad boy. But she's no longer sweet and innocent. And she has a score to settle with him. One that won't be paid until he's hot, bothered and begging for more.

HBCNMBPA0309